Any Two
Can Play

Any Two Can Play

Elizabeth Cadell

G.K. Hall & Co. • **Chivers Press**
Thorndike, Maine USA   Bath, England

This Large Print edition is published by G.K. Hall & Co., USA
and by Chivers Press, England.

Published in 2000 in the U.S. by arrangement with
Brandt & Brandt Literary Agency.

Published in 2000 in the U.K. by arrangement with
Raymond Reynolds and Caroline Cadell.

U.S. Hardcover   0-7838-8837-6   (Romance Series)
U.K. Hardcover   0-7540-4037-2   (Chivers Large Print)
U.K. Softcover   0-7540-4038-0   (Camden Large Print)

Copyright © 1981 by Elizabeth Cadell

G.K. Hall Large Print Romance Series.

The text of this Large Print edition is unabridged.
Other aspects of the book may vary from the original edition.

Set in 16 pt. Plantin by Al Chase.

Printed in the United States on permanent paper.

British Library Cataloguing-in-Publication Data available

Library of Congress Cataloging-in-Publication Data
Cadell, Elizabeth.
    Any two can play / by Elizabeth Cadell.
        p.   cm.
    ISBN 0-7838-8837-6 (lg. print : hc : alk. paper)
    1. Large type books.   I. Title.
PR6005.A225 A83 2000
823´.914—dc21   99-054770

Any Two Can Play

Chapter

1

The lift sped silently to the seventh floor, and Natalie Travers stepped out and pressed the doorbell of apartment number 71. A voice issued from the speaker beside it.

"Who is it?"

"Natalie."

"Darling, how lovely!" The high, affected tone came through very clearly. "Come in, will you, and pour yourself a drink. I'll be with you in three minutes."

There was a releasing click. Natalie pushed open the door, closed it after her, hung her coat in the hall and entered the large, beautifully furnished drawing room. She did not get herself a drink; instead, she walked to the wide window and stood looking down at the only thing about this luxurious apartment that she liked: its view over the city of London. Beautiful by day, on this clear October night it was breathtaking.

Her sister-in-law, approaching noiselessly across the deep carpet, was suddenly at her side.

"Sorry I wasn't ready, darling. But you were just a fraction early, weren't you?"

"Possibly." Natalie turned and dropped a kiss on the other woman's proffered cheek. "Hello, Freddie. How's everything?"

"Everything's fine. Maurice should be here in a moment. He had a shower and changed when he got home from the office, but then he had to go down two floors to say some rude things to a man who's taken to hogging his place in the car park. What a nice dress. You made it?"

"No."

Freddie, who was wearing an expensive creation made in the current kaftan mode, gave an envious sigh.

"I thought it was one of those little numbers you run up. I wish I could do it. Think of the pounds I'd save."

Natalie thought of them and multiplied them by some hundreds. She knew where her sister-in-law bought her clothes.

Freddie had been christened Winifred, but in her early teens had changed this label for one she considered more suited to her personality. She was tall and in a severe way handsome, with a figure as slim as constant calorie-counting could keep it. Her age was the subject of some speculation among her acquaintances. She admitted to thirty-seven.

"A drink?" She was at a side table on which bottles and glasses were set out. "You like sherry, don't you?"

"Please."

Natalie, sipping it, recognized it as the second-best sherry and thought that it was salutary to pay an occasional visit to Maurice and Freddie. Not a word said, but their assessment of your

8

social slot made only too clear.

She waited for Freddie to pour herself out vodka and then followed her to a sofa.

"Maurice is going to talk seriously to you, Natalie." Freddie's tone had changed; it was now crisp, an indication that the courtesies had been completed and business had begun. "He's terribly worried about you, and so am I. We both think you're making a great mistake in going to Downing. Once you get there, you'll find yourself trapped. We all know Julian; he'll simply hand you the problem and leave you to cope with it. He'll wash his hands of the whole thing. He went into it with his eyes wide open, and this is the result. I warned him, when he said he was going to marry that awful girl, that he was running into trouble; I told him that her oh-look-silly-little-me-I've-gone-and-got-pregnant act was as old as time, and, anyway, didn't mean a thing these days. It was simply a tryout to see if he'd marry her."

"But she *was* pregnant."

"Naturally. She'd thought it all out. And now she's left him with year-old twins and it serves him right and he has no business to drag you into it. But you'll go; that's you all over. You sometimes make me want to scream, you're so ready to let yourself be morally blackmailed. Look at the way you let your mother go on living with you after your father died. She was as strong as a horse and she had friends galore and she could have afforded to get herself into a nice comfort-

9

able home. It isn't even as if she'd wanted to stay with you in that rambling great house. What she wanted was to live with Maurice and me, and if I hadn't fought it, she would have moved in. When I'd finally convinced her that it wasn't on, she went back to you, and you acted the dutiful daughter. Now you're preparing to act the dutiful sister. Maurice is going to tell you exactly what he thinks about it. And here he is, so he can start talking."

She got up and went to the door to meet the well-built, handsome man who came into the room. He patted her shoulder, said, "Ring for dinner, Freddie, will you?" and went over to greet Natalie.

"Nice to see you." He bent and kissed her cheek. "Give me your glass, and I'll top it up. How's the career of rent collector going?"

"It's a bit too early to say. The last tenant only moved in two months ago, and there are still one or two things to be done to the rooms."

"Do you regret having given up your teaching job?"

"No."

"Let's hope your tenants pay up regularly. Wait till I tell you what happened to those people who let the house they bought from Freddie's father. Or have you told her, Freddie?"

"No. I haven't had time; she's only just got here. Do I have time for another drink before they send up dinner?"

Her husband brought it to her, and while he

told Natalie the story of the tenants, Freddie studied her sister-in-law with an irritation she found it difficult to conceal. Ever since their first meeting, Natalie had puzzled and confused her. Moving as she herself did in a circle within which fashionable trends, however bizarre, were faithfully followed, she was unable to understand Natalie's indifference to changes in modes or manners. Take that dress: wrong length. That hairstyle: wrong cut. Cosmetics, if any, far too lightly applied; any beautician could have told her that ash blondes needed toning up. You had to admit that she had a lovely face and figure, but why did she persist in leaving them as they were? Freddie felt strongly that a natural appearance was only permissible, only really effective, if it was artificially produced. The thing that most exasperated her, however, was the fact that without a thought for her appearance, without making any effort to please, Natalie exercised a potent attraction on almost every man who met her. And then? No response, no follow-up; not a sign of reciprocal interest. Well, time had a way of marching on. In three years she'd be thirty; somebody ought to tell her that men might get tired of trying.

Maurice had finished with tenants and was giving his views on package tourists, who, he complained, now infested places which had formerly been reserved for himself and his friends. Natalie, half listening, watched him and thought that each time she met him, he seemed to have grown more assertive. They did not meet often; she disliked Freddie and had become adept at evading her frequent invitations. She had retained a mild sisterly affection for Maurice, but there was too much difference in their ages — he was a month off forty — for her to have known him well. Though it might, she thought, be nothing to do with age; Julian was only four years younger than Maurice, but she had always found him easier to get on with. Perhaps it was the fact that Maurice had never had much time to give to family relationships, being dedicated to the pursuit of money. He had made it and he had married it and the chase was still continuing. Julian's only ambitions, now realized, had been to work in a musical world and spend his leisure hours on a golf course.

Through the arch separating drawing room from dining room Natalie could see a long table spread with a lacy pale green tablecloth. On this were the dark green plates used for informal meals. The Meissen china was brought out when Maurice and Freddie entertained the useful contacts they called friends. Tall candles waited to be lit. Maurice went in and put a match to them and stood ready to pull out his wife's chair.

"A very simple meal, Natalie darling," Freddie said as she took her place. "Roast chicken and fresh fruit salad — all right?"

Natalie, aware that this was not a caviar occasion, said that roast chicken sounded very nice.

The apartment block provided a direct connection to the kitchens of the ground-floor restaurant. Maurice slid open the door of the service hatch, took out heavy plated dishes and put them on a hot plate on the sideboard. He served his wife and sister and then carried his own portion to the table.

"Shouldn't lecture you while you're eating," he told Natalie, "but I'm not going to let you get embroiled in this mess of Julian's if I can help it. He's only got himself to blame."

"Exactly the words I used," Freddie said. "But awful as his wife was, I don't know how she managed to stand life with a selfish beast like Julian for as long as a year. I would have packed up after the first month. Half the time, I don't suppose he knew she was there at all; he was too busy forming school orchestras or conducting school orchestras or sending school orchestras to perform abroad and boost the sacred name of the school. In his free time he'd probably walk up to the golf course to have a session with the pro. Do you know" — she turned to Natalie — "we wouldn't have known a thing about his wife leaving him if Maurice hadn't run into someone who knew him? This man said that Julian had told him that his wife had walked out and left him to cope with the twins, but it was all right because his sister had agreed to come and take over. You hadn't said a word about it, so Maurice got in touch with you at once and got you here to tell you that you weren't to let yourself be victimized."

"How much did Julian tell you?" Maurice asked Natalie.

"Not much. He said she was waiting for him when he got home on Friday evening, and then she picked up her suitcase and walked out and drove away in her Mini. She'd sent her heavy luggage away, and she'd taken everything that belonged to her."

"And a lot of things that didn't, I bet," said Freddie. "What did she have when she married him? Not a thing."

"What I can't see," said Maurice, "is why he couldn't find someone in Downing to take over. It isn't a village; it's a sizable town, and he's been living in it for the past three years. Don't tell me there wasn't somebody he could have got hold of, some woman, the wife or the daughter of one of his colleagues, to go in and help. Suppose you'd still had Mother alive and on your hands? Suppose you'd still been teaching? Suppose you hadn't converted the house and still had the whole of it to cope with? Suppose for any other reason you hadn't been free to go? Then what?"

"She married him," said Freddie, "because she thought your mother was rich and would leave him a lot of money. Well, your mother wasn't and didn't, and I'm certain that ever since that will was read five months ago, Julian's wife has been planning to get away and find herself another man."

There was a pause; they waited for Natalie to say something.

"I don't mind anything," she said, "but those two babies. How she could —"

"All Freddie and I are concerned with," Maurice broke in, "is to see that you don't get stuck there indefinitely."

"I'll risk a prophecy," Freddie said. "Julian will thank Natalie when she arrives and tell her he'll never cease to be grateful. Then he'll show her where everything is, heave a sigh of relief and put the whole problem out of his mind."

"When did you last see him?" Maurice asked Natalie.

"Ages ago. The twins were about four months old. I drove to Downing for the day."

"Did they ever invite you to go and stay with them?"

"No."

"They didn't invite us, either. Now he's only too keen to get you there. I agree with Freddie: Once he's got over the relief of seeing you, he'll leave you to get on with it. You're a fool to go, but I suppose it's too late to stop you. If we've put you on your guard, that's something. Freddie and I talked it over and we think . . ."

There followed a good deal of what they thought. Maurice let Freddie do most of the talking, for he was beginning to have the uncomfortable feeling that Natalie, outwardly all polite attention, was not listening to a word. There was something in her manner, something he could not put his finger on, that seemed to mock his pronouncements. He felt injured; hadn't he always been ready to guide her, advise her, influence her? She had shown no desire to be guided or advised or influenced, but he had gone on trying. He had introduced more than one of his men friends to her — not that she lacked men friends, but the men she knew and the men he and Freddie knew were in rather different financial brackets. Any girl but this one would have been grateful for his brotherly interest — but he had begun to realize lately that nothing he said had the smallest effect on her. Worse, she gave him the feeling that something about him amused her.

She had, he knew, an independent streak. Their father had left her the large, outdated family house in Brighton. He himself was married, living and working in London. Julian was musical director at Downinghurst, the famous public school in Kent. They had both urged her to sell; the house was far too large for her, and its key position in the town gave it a considerable value. But she had elected to go on living in it. On their mother's death, Natalie had used her capital to convert the house into self-contained apartments, all but one of which — her own — were now let. And this she had done, he mused resentfully, without so much as a word to himself and Freddie. Or, so far as he knew, to Julian.

It was of Julian that Natalie was thinking now. Julian was in difficulties. He had often been in difficulties before. Their mother had helped him out more than once with money. Maurice had been ready with advice. She herself had given what practical help she could. She had disliked and distrusted the girl he married — but she was bearing his children, and he seemed willing to accept parental responsibilities. Now the marriage was over, but the twins remained.

If they had been older, or younger, she reflected, things might have been easier. Younger, they could have been left for reasonably long periods in their cots or prams. Older, they might have been able to do something for themselves. But at just over a year old, they were at once mobile and helpless and needed constant overlooking.

On one point — her ability to look after the twins — she knew that neither Freddie nor Maurice could express any doubts. At twenty-seven she had seen many of her friends marry and become parents, and she had frequently undertaken the role of substitute mother. She liked young children, and young children liked her. Life with the egotistical Julian would have its difficult moments, but she did not share Freddie and Maurice's fears about being trapped; she was, on the contrary, confident that she would be able to find in a large town like Downing a pair of competent women to assume charge of Julian's house and children.

Freddie had finished speaking. Maurice put the empty dishes into the hatch and pressed the button that would take them back to the kitchens. The coffee had been bubbling on the sideboard; he blew out the candles and carried the tray into the drawing room, and they settled down to resume their talk. The curtains had been drawn across the archway; Natalie knew that when they were opened again on the following morning, the daily maid would have placed the breakfast things on the table, washed and dried the dinner plates and tidied the drawing room. Life with Freddie, she mused. No cooking, no cleaning, no domestic shopping, no supermarket bags bulging with carrots and potatoes; washing sent down the chute to the laundry. No need to worry about anything except keeping abreast of the latest trends and keeping in with the right set. A nice life — if you could call it living.

Soon after they had finished their coffee, she rose to say good-bye; she had a sixty-mile drive before her.

"I can't see," Maurice said, "why you told Julian you'd go to Downing tonight. You won't get there until the early hours."

"He knows that. He's waiting up for me."

"I don't think you ought to drive by yourself so late," Freddie objected. "Anything might happen."

"Such as?"

"Well, anything. A couple of thugs tried to stop our car the other night when we were driving back from the theater. One of them tried to open the door, but Maurice jabbed him in the face and drove straight on. If we had a bed to offer you, I'd make you stay, and then you could go in the morning."

No bed. Natalie smiled to herself. Only two bedrooms. Only two bathrooms. Only two vast sofas. But nowhere to put visitors.

"I'll enjoy the drive," she said. "Thank you for the nice dinner."

Freddie said good-bye at the door. Maurice walked to the lift and put a question as they waited for it.

"You know that Michael Morley will soon be back?"

"Yes."

"I suppose he's kept in touch with you?"

"Yes."

"Is he . . . Are you . . . I don't want to butt in, of course, but he's been keen on you for a long time. You know he's come into his uncle's money?"

"And title. Yes."

"Freddie thinks he'd suit you very well — and I wouldn't mind seeing you married to him, They're a good family."

"I know."

She got into the lift. Maurice returned to Freddie to sum up the evening.

"Waste of time," he said.

"I knew it would be. But I was right to make you ask her and put on a big-brother act. Now she can't say you didn't show some interest. Did you ask her about Michael Morley?"

"Yes."

"What did she say?"

"Nothing."

"If she lets him go, I'm not going to let you line up any more men for her to turn down. Don't stay up too long; I'm sleepy."

Left alone, he poured himself out a whisky nightcap and congratulated himself on having had the sense to marry Freddie. She had her faults — who hadn't? — but she had kept him moving in the right direction and had steered him away from some tricky situations. And she had put down a firm foot whenever he had looked like being talked into anything rash, as, for instance, when his mother had pressed for a joint establishment. Yes, Freddie used her head. You had to give her her due.

Natalie, driving through the night, was also giving Freddie her due. She'd taken on a somewhat homespun Maurice and turned him into a glossy showpiece. She'd crossed swords with their formidable mother and defeated her. She had been two years older than Maurice when she married him and was now three years younger. Formidable, was Freddie.

She tried to assess how much affection she still had for either of her brothers and came to the conclusion that it was not a great deal. Their father had been the only member of the family with whom she had been in sympathy, the only one who took life lightly or had any touch of humour.

The lights in Julian's house were on when she

reached it at half past one. His station wagon was at the door, and she parked her car behind it. The curtains of the two front rooms were undrawn, and she could see clearly the untidy state of the interior.

London to Downing. Maurice and Freddie to Julian. Not much in the way of mileage, but an unbridgeable gap between two totally dissimilar ways of life.

Julian opened the door as she reached it. The hall light silhouetted his figure, taller and leaner than Maurice's. She stepped inside, and his feature became visible, his eyes behind his glasses blinking and sleep-filled. The familiar strand of hair hung over his forehead. He spoke in his slow, unemphatic way.

"Thought you wouldn't come," he said as he took her suitcase and closed the door.

"Why? I said I would."

"You also said you were dining with Maurice. I thought he and his frightful Freddie would talk you out of it. I bet they did their best."

Natalie let this pass. He and his brother, as schoolboys, had been good friends. Since then they had been moving steadily apart. Maurice's marriage had widened the breach; Julian's had made it impassable.

"I left the garage for you. Why didn't you put your car in?"

"No need."

They were edging round the double pram in the hall. Julian ushered her into the drawing room.

21

"Come into the piggery," he invited.

It was a fair description. Babies' garments hung on sofas and chairs. Bottles, jars, tins of baby food stood on mantelpiece and windowsill. Music sheets lay on the floor beside the open piano. The remnants of a meal were on the table.

"We turned this into a kind of living room," he explained. "It was too much fuss to use two big rooms, so we left the dining room and moved in here. I meant to do a bit of tidying-up before you arrived but didn't have time. Then I fell asleep on the sofa. Want anything to eat?"

"No, thanks."

"Drink?"

"I wouldn't mind something hot. I'll make it. How are the twins?"

"They're all right. I tried to find someone for the job, Natalie, I honestly did. I did everything short of advertising. I haunted the labour exchange, and I harassed all my friends. But who'd want to take on year-old twins, a largish house and man who's very seldom in it? The very idea made people laugh. In the end, the mother of one of the choirboys came round and said she was a retired nurse and had heard I was in difficulties, and she offered to look after the twins for a few days, until you came. Her name's Mrs. Gilling. She wouldn't do anything in the house, and she said I'd have to look after myself."

They had moved to the kitchen. Natalie was heating water to make coffee. The sink was full of unwashed plates, but the bowls and cups used by the twins had been washed and neatly stacked. The stove was stained and smelled of milk that had boiled over and been left to dry.

"There's a list of the twins' menus hanging on the door," Julian said. "Mrs. Gilling seemed efficient, so I left her to it. I couldn't have stayed round because she never stopped talking — on and on and on. You'll find out soon; she'll be coming to see you."

"It was nice of her to help out."

"So I told her. But the fact is that she gets most of her pleasure in life by minding other people's business." He pulled out a chair and sat down. "I suppose you want to know if the twins miss their mother?"

"Well, do they?"

"No, they don't. They didn't see enough of her to get to know her well. One thing about twins: they're company for each other."

"Do you know where she went?"

"Yes. Back to London. She said she was sorry she ever left it. She never shed the illusion that if you don't live in a capital city, you're missing out on culture. So she's gone back, and I suppose she'll get a job and find a man, only this time it'll be sex without strings."

"I don't see why she had children. Freddie still says it was to —"

"— make her marry me. That's not the only one of Freddie's ideas that wants the cobwebs brushed off it. The reason she wanted children was to prove how easy it was for an intelligent woman to make a success of two simultaneous careers. That Oxford degree of hers went to her head. She claimed she could run husband and home with one hand and rock a political cradle with the other. She had the theories all worked out, but they fell down when she put them into practice. She found out that the twins were real. They howled; they made messes; they needed changing. She was annoyed at the discovery that a husband came home hungry and expected to be fed, that a house needed an occasional workover with a broom or a duster. At last she understood that she'd talked herself into a trap, and began looking for a way out."

"Why did she agree to live here?"

"My job was here. This house was here, rent-free. She could have made friends here if she hadn't made it clear to everybody that she didn't consider them up to her intellectual standard. There are people in this town with a whole lot more brains than she's got, but she lumped them together as peasants."

"Was she ever in love with you?"

"No. I think she thought I was good molding material — until she found I wasn't. The whole thing happened too fast for me. I was only in London for those few weeks, guest conducting, and I came back married and a prospective father. She had other men around — I don't know why she picked me for the big experiment. Well, now it's folded, and I'm grateful to you for coming to pick up the pieces."

"Do you think she'll come back?"

"No. Never. She's had enough. And so," he added, "have I." He paused. "People expect me to go round looking embittered, but if you want the truth, I'm glad she went. In a way, I feel sorry for her. She's going to have to reassess her intellectual level. In London she was in a set of those left-wingers who are so good at talking. My God, could they talk! Some of them knew what they were talking about, but I began to realize that most of what was said was secondhand. She got past because she looked brainy — weird clothes and thick glasses and a donnish manner — but I think she's reached her academic ceiling, and not a high ceiling at that. And that's all about her and me. How about Maurice? Still pleased with his dolly-wife?"

"Yes. They've moved to —"

"I know. One of those blocks in which the tenants only have to breathe in and breathe out, and the buttons take care of the rest. I don't know how Maurice can shut himself into one of those biscuit tins. God, what a pair! They haven't even got a poodle that he can take for walks in the park. She rang up about two months ago and said she was driving through Downing and might drop in. I said we wouldn't be here."

"Why? It was a friendly overture."

"Friendly overture, my foot. It was an itch to look us over and report back to headquarters. And now we come to you. Has coming here disrupted anything?"

"No."

"How long can you stay?"

She smiled.

"Until you manage to fill the post satisfactorily."

"It's not going to be easy to find anyone in this place."

"Have you really tried?"

"I told you — I asked everyone. No result."

"It's a big town. We'll see what advertising can do."

She had spoken tranquilly. He stared at her with a frown for some moments, and then she saw his expression undergoing a gradual change. The look of strain left his face. The frown vanished. She knew that he had done what all his life he had been in the habit of doing: he had handed over the load. He had shed the burden, put the problem away. From now on he would leave someone else — in the present case, herself — to do the worrying. She had always thought of it as his vanishing trick.

"Your tenants paying up?" he asked.

"Yes."

"I suppose converting the house ate up all your capital?"

"Most of it. But I'm getting rent from five sets of tenants and living rent-free myself."

"What about your teaching job? Will you go back to it?"

"Probably."

"How about your love life?"

"Same as usual, I think."

"That fellow — what's his name? Morley — is he still hanging round you?"

"He went to Kuala Lumpur. He's due back soon."

"Is he one of the chaps that Maurice and Freddie lined up for you?"

"Yes."

"Are you going to marry him?"

"No."

"Well, I don't want to sound like Maurice, but I feel it's time you made up your mind. God knows you've had enough choice."

"That's Freddie's view, too. Watch that kettle, will you? I'm going up to look at the twins."

"You needn't go quietly; they're tight sleepers. Your room is the spare bedroom over-looking the front. About food, there isn't much in the house. I've been living on Indian or Chinese take-aways. I could order —"

"I'll manage. Watch the kettle."

She found the children's room, with its wide cot for two, as untidy as the rooms downstairs. But nothing could detract from the peace and beauty of the two small sleeping forms. Boy and girl: Randall and Rowena, both fair like herself, both with Julian's features. They lay head to toe on the rumpled sheet, the blanket a ball between them. She unrolled it, turned Rowena gently round, laid the blanket over them and tucked it in. Then she went into the spare bedroom. The bed was unmade, but someone, Julian or Mrs. Gilling, had put out clean bedclothes.

The sound of the kettle boiling over made her return hurriedly to the kitchen. She found hot water spurting over the counter, and switched off the current. The kettle had been a gift from herself and, when new, had turned itself off automatically, but she was soon to discover that it was only one of many things in this house that had been misused and left unrepaired.

She was about to make two cups of coffee when the total silence in the drawing room made her go in to investigate. Sprawled on the sofa lay Julian, fast asleep.

She stood looking down at him. He looked younger than his years, and deceptively vulnerable. Their mother's pet, their father's pride. A good pianist, an exceptionally good flautist, a bad golfer, an indifferent brother. A man whose gentle, rather hesitating charm led strangers to the mistaken belief that he was unsure of himself.

Music was more than his work. It was also his hobby; in a sense it was his mission. He believed that anybody who was not tone-deaf could be turned into a performer. The greatest pleasure for the true music lover, he said, was in do-it-yourself. You didn't have to aim at being a virtuoso; all you had to do was fix on an instrument and play it at whatever level of accomplishment.

He had come to Downinghurst three years ago and for the first time in his teaching career had been given a free hand. The school now had two full and four chamber orchestras — but his search for talent still went on. Boys and girls of all ages were cajoled into scraping, blowing or banging, and sat with their unfamiliar instruments before music stands, their eyes moving frenziedly between bar and baton.

Music for his spirit, Natalie reflected. Golf for his legs and lungs. And to free him from domestic responsibilities, a convenient sister . . .

She went back to the kitchen, drank her coffee and then, resisting a strong impulse to initiate some form of tidying, picked up her suitcase and went upstairs to bed.

Chapter

2

She slept soundly. Since she always rose early, there had been no need to set her alarm. While she was dressing, the sound of a car made her go to the window, and she was in time to see Julian driving away to get in an early game of golf.

It was the first time she had seen the view from an upper window, and she stood admiring it. The house was one of a widely spaced row built along a lane that marked the present perimeter of the town. These houses had been erected about twenty years ago, when the golf course had been added to the town's amenities. She could see the course in the distance beyond the fields, green and undulating and edged with tall trees. Encircling the house was a small garden which neither Julian nor his wife had troubled to cultivate. She could not see the houses on the left of this one, but to the right, one was visible: a small, trim, single-storied cottage partly screened by a hedge and surrounded by flowering shrubs. She could see a narrow path ending in a low wooden gate and the window of an uncurtained side room, furnished but seemingly unoccupied.

From the twins' room came gurgles. She went in and saw them lying on top of the blanket, engaged in a wrestling match. They broke off to stare long and intently at her; she stood by the cot, giving them time to make their assessment, and then began to play with them. When good relations had been established, she washed and dressed them and left them in the cot while she went downstairs to prepare their meal and her own.

Julian had had nothing but coffee. A note propped against the milk jug stated that he would not be back for breakfast and that he always lunched at the school. She read the chart of instructions hanging on the door, prepared food and milk for the twins, made her coffee, pulled up the twins' high chairs and then went upstairs to fetch them.

However disturbed their background might have been, she reflected as she fed them, they appeared to be healthy and happy. Randall was clearly the leader; Rowena merely copied everything he did. He was under the impression that he could talk fluently, and used the intervals between mouthfuls to make loud and impassioned speeches. She thought that perhaps, like his uncle Maurice, he had political ambitions.

It was a beautiful morning, sunny, with air that felt almost mild. When the twins had finished their breakfast, she put their playpen out on the balcony that opened from the dining room, lifted them into it, surrounded them with toys and then went to work on the house. For the next two hours, with brief interruptions to visit the twins, she cleared and cleaned, washed, swept and dusted and had the satisfaction of seeing the house beginning to look as it had perhaps looked when Julian and his wife first came to it.

It was a pleasant house, well furnished and equipped. It had been allocated to the head of the School of Arts inaugurated in the town — but this had proved an over-ambitious project, and the authorities had decided to close it. The main building had been bought by the school, Downinghurst, as a Music Department. Julian, the school's senior music master, was given a rise in salary and status, together with the house that had been intended for the head of the Arts School. The fact that it was situated, at some distance from the town center was of no importance, since the school buildings were scattered, university-fashion, all over the town.

At about half past eleven Natalie took milk and biscuits to the twins on the balcony and found the sun so warm that she removed the children's woolen sweaters. She had found nothing in the kitchen that she could use for her lunch. It would have been sensible, she thought, to have driven herself and the twins into town and bought some stores.

As she was turning over this course in her mind, a large car, built for space rather than style, drove up and stopped outside. From the driving seat struggled a very stout, motherly-looking woman of about fifty whose attire seemed designed specifically for between-seasons: a heavy tweed suit to resist the chill of autumn, but a thin cotton blouse and beach sandals in case summer lingered. When Natalie opened the door, she began to speak in a voice loud and flavoured with a west-country accent, her words pouring out with scarcely a pause for breath.

"My goodness, I'm glad you've come! I'm Mrs. Gilling. I've been holding the fort till you got here, and it hasn't been easy, I can tell you, but I felt I had to do it. I've got a house of my own to run, to say nothing of a husband and two schoolboy sons, but I couldn't leave your brother and those poor little mites without help."

"You've been very kind. Please come in."

"I saw him as he was driving to the school this morning, and he told me you'd arrived, and all I've looked in for now is to say I'm going to the shops and I'll leave some stores in his car and he can bring them home with him, just to start you off, because I know there's nothing in the house and you couldn't be expected to dash off shopping until you'd had time to turn round. Your brother eats out, mostly, but I don't suppose you need telling that he's not a man who worries much about household matters."

By the end of this speech she had followed Natalie into the hall, negotiated the double pram and made her way through the dining room to the balcony.

"*There* you are, my sweeties," she shouted, bending affectionately over the twins. "All nice and clean and tidy, with your nice auntie to look after you." She turned her blue, slightly protruding, good-natured gaze towards the dining room. "Clean and tidy indeed," she said admiringly. "How did you get all that cleaning-up done? You must have been all night at it. It's the first time I've ever been able to make out the pattern on that carpet. I don't know what opinion you had of your sister-in-law, but let me tell you . . . Yes, thanks, I'd love a cup of coffee if it's made, don't bother if it isn't. I must tell you that . . . My word, just look at this kitchen! You've done wonders, you really have. It was a shame to let a nice house like this go to seed the way she did. You didn't know her very well, did you?"

"No."

"I thought not. I'm going by the way you came here only once, and your other brother never came at all, so I guessed how things were. Mind you, people here like your brother very much; they think he's done wonders for the school in the music line. But as for her! A lovely pair of babies like those, and no idea in her head but to get away from them. Men shouldn't marry women like her; it's not fair on the children. Your poor brother didn't have much of a life. We all think it was wicked to walk out the way she did, but now you're here, it'll be all right. You've had a lot of experience running a house, haven't you? You lived with your mother, wasn't that it?

And she died six months ago, that's right, isn't it?"

"Five."

"Then you turned your house into flats and you've let them and you're looking after the tenants. Well, I hope they can look after themselves for a while. This is very good coffee. I'm not much of a hand at making it. My husband's a tea drinker, and so are the boys. Yes, please, another cup if you can squeeze the pot. The thing we've got to do now is to look round for domestic help. You can leave it to me; I've lived in this town for over twenty years, and I know where to look for people. And now I ought to be going. It's a funny thing, we don't get much excitement in this place as a rule, but lately there's been a lot. There was your brother's wife going off, for a start, and then there was the news about Miss Downing — the youngest one, Blanche. I suppose your brother told you all about that."

"No."

"Well, he hasn't had time, I daresay. But everybody's pleased. Well, nearly everybody. Some's hinting that she's been married for her money because he's coming to live here, in her house. But why not? She'd only just bought it and fixed it up with all her nice furniture she brought from Downing House. Whoever got her has got a prize. She looked after her father more or less on her own, night and day, right up to the time he died. She'll make a good wife. Mark you, she's getting on. She must be the wrong side of

35

sixty, but she doesn't look her age, even though she worked so hard all those years. You know she's your next-door neighbour, don't you?"

"No."

"You can't see much of the house; it's got a good thick hedge. When she'd got it all fixed up, she went off on that cruise where she met her husband. Now she's back. She got here yesterday evening, but nobody's seen her yet, nor him either. And young Mr. Downing's here, though he shouldn't be called young Mr. Downing now that old Mr. Downing's dead, but habit's habit, isn't it? People say he's come to sell the house now that his aunts have moved out of it, so there'll be a clubhouse for the golfers at last, and that'll please them, though I think it's a shame, and so does my husband, to give up a place your ancestors lived in for so long. Sixteen hundred and something, long before this town was thought of. Now I'll have to be on my way; I've got a lot of shopping to do and my husband's waiting for me in town and he doesn't like to be kept waiting; men don't, do they? They're all alike. If you want anything, just give me a ring. And don't think" — she paused at the front door and spoke reassuringly — "don't think I'm going to forget about getting someone to come and work for your brother. I'll do all I can, and I'll keep you in touch."

She got into her car, backed jerkily to the gate and then drove onto the lane and out of sight. Natalie went back to the balcony and, after looking out at the sunny fields, decided to put the twins into their pram and take them for a short walk.

There was a slight check when she put them into the pram — it was the first sign of discontent they had given since they woke. She found the cause to be the fact that Rowena preferred one side of the pram and Randall preferred the other, and no changeover was going to be tolerated. This matter settled, they were ready to ride.

Once in the lane, with the fields on one side and the houses hidden by hedges, Natalie felt that they might have been in open country, far from any town. The sun was disappearing from time to time behind clouds, but there did not seem to be any immediate prospect of rain. She spread a groundsheet and lifted the twins onto it and, seated with her back to a tree, sat watching them crawling in chase of one another. Rowena, she saw, was making efforts to walk, but Randall preferred proceeding on all fours.

There was nobody in sight except, in the distance, golfers moving slowly across the course, pausing to play a stroke and moving on again. She watched them lazily, content for the moment to put aside Julian's problems — and her own.

She had come here in answer to an appeal, but she was not sorry to be away from home for a time. Since her decision to convert her house, she had had to endure, day after day and week after week, the sounds of sawing and hammering. She had made countless cups of tea for plumbers and carpenters and electricians; she had cooked and eaten and slept with the dust of demolition thick in the air. Now the work was over, the tenants were in, her own small apartment was ready and she could use this interlude to decide what she was going to do with her life.

She would have liked to marry. She had seen a good deal of the advantages and disadvantages of the married state and had come to the conclusion that it was on the whole the best way of life for a woman who liked children as much as she did. But it took two to make a marriage, and she had not yet met a man with whom she felt she could settle down. She knew that she was beginning to be regarded by her friends as too hard to please; she had been unable to tell them exactly what she wanted in a husband — but she knew very well what she did not want.

She came back to the present to find that something had drawn the children's attention. Following their gaze, she saw a man approaching from the direction in which she and the twins had come. He was carrying golf clubs and was walking towards the road that connected the course with the town. He would have to pass her. She drew the groundsheet and the twins aside to give him room. As he came nearer, she saw that he was dark-haired, with a long, lean face she thought attractive. He looked a few years younger than Julian. He was walking slowly, his gaze on the distant golf course, obviously deep in thought — or in dreams.

As he reached the group, Rowena decided to take a walk. She pushed herself upright, staggered a few steps and collapsed at the feet of the stranger. Attempting to save herself, she stretched out her arms and hooked them firmly round the man's leg. Brought up in mid-step, he executed a series of hops, failed to regain his balance and measured his length on the ground. The twins sat expectant, awaiting developments.

The man got to his feet, dusted his trousers and picked up his golf clubs.

"I'm sorry." Natalie broke the uncomfortable silence. "You should have stopped before she grabbed you."

He studied her with raised eyebrows for a moment or two and then turned to address Rowena.

"There's a nice park for children in the town," he told her mildly. "With more people to give you tackling practice."

"Did you hurt yourself?" Natalie inquired.

His eyes came back to her. There was a gleam in them — whether of anger or humour she could not decide.

"Thank you for asking," he said. "No, I didn't."

"It wouldn't have happened if you hadn't been dreaming."

"It wouldn't have happened if you'd been in the park. This, if I may mention the fact, is a private road reserved for the residents of the houses along it. Are you a resident?"

"No. Is there a notice?"

"There will be tomorrow. And I wasn't dreaming. I was grappling with a problem." He bent and shook Rowena's hand. "Good-bye. No hard feelings. Ask your mother to take you to that nice park."

He walked on. She saw him stop some distance away at a gate that opened onto the golf course. He took a key from his pocket, let himself through and locked the gate after him. He had not looked back since passing her.

She was left with a faint sense of disappointment. It was a pity Rowena had got in his way. She had liked the look of him and would have enjoyed talking to him for a while. But nobody could expect a man to stop for a friendly chat when he had been deposited nose down in the dust.

She looked at her watch. It was just after twelve — time to take the twins home and feed them. When she reached the house, she was surprised to see Julian's car. He came out and helped her lift the pram into the hall and explained his unexpected appearance.

"I got a phone call from the headmaster. He had something he wanted to talk over with me, so I asked him to come here. Eating at the school means getting involved with too many people and getting nothing fixed. I offered him beer and sandwiches. There's ham and some stores on the kitchen table — Mrs. Gilling put them into my car. Could you . . . would you mind —"

"— making the sandwiches? No. But I'll get the twins' food first. Then you can feed them while I cut the bread."

He lifted the children onto their chairs.

"I thought of stopping on the way home to put an ad in the local paper," he said. "But I didn't, because I couldn't decide on the wording. 'Wanted, nanny for year-old twins, must also be good cook and efficient housekeeper.' If I put that in, I'd have members of the women's militant movements stoning me in the streets."

"There's another approach," Natalie suggested. " 'An attractive male, good musician, keen golfer, seeks tall blonde with similar tastes, must be child lover.' But I agree — it's difficult."

"It wouldn't have been, not so long ago," Julian complained. "What became of all those women they used to call spinsters, who went on the hunt for husbands?"

"They're the ones who'd do the stoning. You've eaten two sandwiches. Why didn't you have breakfast?"

"I did. Eggs and bacon at a café in town. I wish we could get a clubhouse on the course. All we've ever had is a small wooden hut. We've been hoping for years to buy Downing House, but —"

"Where's Downing House?"

"On the far side of the course. You can't see it — it's screened by those trees you can see in the distance. The Downing family lived in it for centuries — since sixteen hundred and something; thirty, I think. It was the park surrounding the house that the town bought and turned into a golf course. They thought they were going to be able to buy the house, too, but old man Downing decided to go on living in it."

"He's dead, Mrs. Gilling said."

"Yes. A few months ago. But when he died, his three elderly daughters were still living in the house and looked like staying there till they died. The only reason they got out was that their last tottering old retainer announced that he was retiring. The place was too big for them to manage without servants, and getting servants . . . well, you're going to find out."

"Blanche got married."

"I see Mrs. Gilling's been briefing you. Yes, Blanche got married."

"What happened to the other two?"

"They're called Clarice and Geraldine. They're about ten years older than Blanche. They've installed themselves in one of the hotel cottages. They don't speak to Blanche."

"Why not?"

"They accuse her of running out on them. Which I think is exactly what she did. She'd had them round her neck for years. When the retainer left, she bought the house next door to this one, put her furniture in and then shut it up and went on a cruise. Then she wrote to the headmaster, who's an old friend, and said she'd met a nice, mature, sensible man on board and they were going to be married. Then a two-line announcement in the *Times*: 'In London, quietly, Blanche Downing to Marcus Wray.' "

"He'd have to be mature. Mrs. Gilling said she was in her sixties."

"Sixty-one, I think. She . . . Here's the head. Come and meet him."

The headmaster, Mr. Whitestone, was a giant of a man, with bushy whiskers framing a tanned, rubbery-looking face. From the forest issued a booming voice that Natalie thought must strike terror into any erring juniors. He brought a huge hand down affectionately on Julian's shoulder and then turned to Natalie.

"Glad we've met at last," he said. "You've come on a rescue operation, but we're not going to let you devote all your time to the twins. We'll have to find you some amusement, won't we, Julian? There are several unmarried schoolmasters, but from the look of you, I'd say there were already a number of bees round the honeypot. I'm sorry to take up Julian's lunch hour, but there was something I wanted to discuss, and if we meet in town or have lunch at the school, we don't get anything said."

"Beer and sandwiches," Natalie said. "I'll take the twins up for their rest, and —"

"— and while you're doing that, Julian and I can chat, and then we'll eat. Fine, fine."

When she came downstairs again, she arranged the sandwiches on a large dish, put beer and glasses onto a wagon and wheeled it into the drawing room. Julian opened bottles and the headmaster leaned back in the largest chair, legs outstretched, comfortable and at ease.

"I've been talking to Julian about this lecture he's giving on Thursday." Like Randall, he interspersed large mouthfuls of food with conversation. "First time we're using the new concert hall."

"What's the lecture on?"

"On orchestras," Julian answered. "With recorded excerpts from great works played by great orchestras."

"His idea being," supplemented the headmaster, "that each orchestra, under a great conductor, gives a different interpretation. I hope he can prove it."

"It's a pretty big hall to fill," Julian pointed out.

"We'll fill it. We'll march the fourth formers and upwards in, and that'll only leave room for the staff and a few outsiders. Miss Travers, you must make Julian take you over some of the school buildings."

"Please call me Natalie."

"Thank you. A nice name. My mother's. Julian, do you know what the school numbers are up to?"

"Over a thousand?"

"No. You're thinking of the fees. God only knows how the unfortunate parents manage to pay them. The local parents are privileged, of course; they get a considerable knock-off. No wonder the population of this town keeps rising. Numbers in the school? When I took over, Natalie, there were four hundred and thirty boys. Then I let the girls in. Now we're coeducational and up to nine hundred and twenty-eight. When we reach the thousand mark — and it won't be long — I'm retiring." He reached out and helped himself to another sandwich. "I've seen a lot of changes in this town, one way and another. That golf course, chiefly. When the town bought Downing Park and its surrounding land and made the course, I worried a bit, and so did my wife. We both thought that too much money had been spent on a privileged section of the community. So much expenditure, to benefit so small a proportion of the townspeople. And at the time we were right because the proportion of golfers was small. But in no time, what happened? Everybody was out on the course practising drives. Which seems to prove that if you provide a golf course, you create a golfing community, and not the other way round."

"Henry Downing's here," Julian said. "I hope he's come to arrange the sale of the house."

"That may be one reason," the headmaster said, "but he's also here because he brought his young half-brother over from Italy. He's now a pupil at the school."

Julian raised his eyebrows.

"I didn't know —"

"You didn't know we were going to have the

honour of educating yet another Downing. I didn't mention it before because it was hanging in the balance — his mother was dead against it. But Henry overruled her."

"Is he the only child?"

"Of the second marriage, yes. Old man Downing," the headmaster explained to Natalie, "had three daughters and one son. The son married a girl from Norfolk, and they had one son — Henry. But Henry's father didn't get on with the old man, so when his wife died, he went to live in Italy. He took Henry with him, but sent him to Downinghurst to be educated. Then he married a second wife — Italian. This youngster, who's called Leonardo, is the result. I thought Henry would stay in England when his father died, but he didn't. All we've seen of him is the occasional glimpse when he's come to England to visit his grandfather or his aunts. I don't know how young Leonardo's going to settle, but I can see Henry's point: he's a Downing and he ought to grow up knowing something about his English background."

"Has he ever been to England before?" Natalie asked.

"Not since his infancy. Being named Leonardo won't do him any good at school, but when I addressed him, tentatively, as Leonard, he corrected me. Very politely. Oh, yes, very politely indeed. He's quite the young patrician. I was rather favourably impressed."

"How old?" Julian asked.

"Eight and a half. If you're wondering whether he's musical, yes. He told me he had a very good voice. He said — I quote — 'I sing very well at present, but perhaps my voice will break.' That sort of remark won't do him any good in the school either. He speaks beautiful English, without a trace of accent — but somehow the foreign intonation's there." He paused. "Speaking of school, Natalie, didn't Julian tell me that you were doing some teaching at one time?"

"I haven't done much lately."

"If I call on you for some coaching help, would you take on one or two of the academic laggards? There'd be no transport problem; they could come and go in the school car, with the school chauffeur. How about it?"

She hesitated.

"I'd be free only when I'd put the twins down for their afternoon rest."

"Two to four?"

"Yes."

"Two to four, say twice a week. Is it a deal?"

"If you like."

"A business deal. My secretary will talk to you about fees. That's fixed, then." He attempted to rise and sank back in his chair. "You've made me too comfortable," he grumbled.

"It's early yet," Julian said.

"For school, yes. But I meant to look in on Miss Downing next door. No, not Miss Downing anymore; Mrs. Wray. I'll never be able to remember. That was good news about her getting married. Unexpected, but good. She could have married more than once in the old days if she hadn't been looking after her father and those two sisters of hers. I don't mind admitting that I went after her myself, in the long, long ago, but her relations made a pretty impenetrable screen. I'm glad she's free of them at last."

"Surely she was free when her father died?" Julian asked.

"No." The headmaster heaved himself to his feet. "No. Make no mistake. When it was clear that they had to get out of Downing House, her sisters, Clarice and Geraldine, took it for granted that the three of them would buy a house in town and settle in it together. They told me so. They told everybody so. They had every intention of going on as they'd always done — leaving Blanche to run the house."

"She sounds the martyr type," Natalie commented.

The headmaster shook his head.

"No, she isn't. It was the war that did it. Her sisters were in their thirties, so they were considered mature enough to go and do war work in the town. Blanche was nineteen, and her parents kept her at home. I think she rather enjoyed it in the beginning — running the house and seeing that her sisters came home to a good dinner after their exhausting job of tying string round parcels for the troops. She enjoyed it less

48

as time went on and all the servants melted away."

"Couldn't the two sisters have given a hand after the war?" Natalie asked.

"No. They decided to stay in town. They'd got a lot of friends there, and they wanted to live there. But the old man thought they should come home, so he stopped their allowance. So they lived at home, but he couldn't stop them from taking jobs and going into town every day. They had no training of any kind, but they pulled a few strings and got the job of looking after the children's department of the public library. It was a job for one person, but they took it on together and shared the salary." He gave a rumbling laugh. "Thirty years they kept that job. They were well over the official retiring age when they gave it up, but they were allowed to stay on because nobody else wanted the job. Nobody wanted to tackle the new generation of young hell raisers. But Clarice and Geraldine gave as good as they got. But they've written off Blanche. When she bought this house next door, they actually proposed to come and share it with her. The only thing that freed her, saved her, was meeting that fellow and marrying him. Now she's safe. She deserves to be happy. Go and visit her while you're here, Natalie. She's never had much opportunity to make friends."

He was at the door, still reluctant to depart.

"Thanks for the beer and the sandwiches and, as they used to say in my youth, thank you for the company. Oh, one other thing, Natalie: you've got to come to that lecture of Julian's. It'll be a good chance to meet some of his colleagues. Don't worry about the twins — I'll send you one of my efficient assistant matrons to take over. In fact, I'll send you young Millie Drew. She's got one or two drawbacks, but she knows her job. Well, good-bye, and thanks again."

Julian watched him drive away and then came back to collect some sheets of music.

"I'll try to get back early," he told Natalie. "Don't do anything about dinner. I pass three take-away restaurants on the way home, and I'll bring back something. How about prawn curry?"

"Sounds nice. But if you want me to cook, I'll cook."

"No. Let's cut out unnecessary chores. Want anything before I go?"

"No, thanks."

He paused in the hall on his way out.

"Take the twins for a walk through the fields," he suggested. "You'll have the landscape all to yourself — nobody goes along there."

"A man went along there this morning. He passed us and then went through the gate onto the golf course."

"He couldn't have done. The Downings are the only people who have a key to that gate. Nobody else . . . but wait a minute. A bit younger than me, dark, tall?"

"Yes."

"Henry Downing. He must have been visiting his aunt Blanche. Did you speak to him?"

"We exchanged a few words. Do you know him?"

"I've met him once or twice when he's been here, but he isn't here often. He drops in and drops out again, fast. Let's hope he'll stay long enough this time to sell his house. If the price doesn't put it out of the reach of the golfers, we'll have a clubhouse at last. See you this evening."

She walked thoughtfully upstairs to get the twins out of bed.

"He wasn't grappling with a problem at all," she told Rowena as she lifted her out of the cot. "He was Henry Downing, of Downing House, Downing, so that's why he had his nose in the air. You were quite right to bring him down to earth."

Chapter

3

For the next few days Natalie found herself fully occupied in looking after the twins, cleaning and polishing, tidying the rest of the house and getting cupboards and drawers into some kind of order. There were no walks with the pram; the weather was cold and misty, and day by day went by without any sign of improvement.

She drove into the town, the twins on their car seat beside her, to lay in stores and institute a regular delivery of milk and bread. Her brief exchanges with the tradespeople revealed the fact that they all regarded her as here to stay. Attempts to convince them that this was a temporary arrangement, that she was here for a short time to fill a gap, met with no success; a replacement, she was told, would be very hard to find. Wasn't Mrs. Gilling doing her best and getting nowhere? Local tongues had been wagging; everybody seemed to know that she drew rents from a property in Brighton, that she was not a novice at housekeeping and that she had at present no plans to marry. The general conclusion was that there was nothing to prevent her from settling down to take charge of her brother's household.

This attitude she saw reflected only too clearly

in Julian. Since conceding that a combined mother-nurse-cook-housekeeper would be difficult to find, he had behaved like one from whom nothing more could be expected. The pleasure and relief he had exhibited on her arrival had evaporated, leaving his normal vague, self-absorbed manner. He assured her that he would look after himself and then departed to the school or to the golf course, leaving his bed unmade, his bedroom in disorder and his washing in a pile on his bathroom floor.

She remembered Maurice's warning and Freddie's advice, but she knew that nothing could have made her change her mind about coming here. She had known Julian's faults too well to need reminding of them — and she had not come on Julian's account. It was the children who had brought her, and they more than compensated for their father's deficiencies. She was already becoming aware that the longer she stayed with them, the harder it was going to be to leave them.

Mrs. Gilling continued to look for domestic assistance, and Natalie was grateful until she realized, as Julian had done, that Mrs. Gilling was by nature a busybody and had found an occupation she enjoyed. She telephoned at frequent intervals and inordinate length to report that she was visiting agencies, alerting friends, questioning acquaintances. The woman in the hairdresser's knew someone . . . a friend had a friend who might . . . Each recital began on a

53

note of confidence and ended in anticlimax. Natalie in desperation attempted to resort to one or other of the conventional means of escape, but found that breaking into one of Mrs. Gilling's monologues to say that something was boiling over, or that someone was ringing the front doorbell, was almost impossible. The only method she found effective was to wait until the river was in spate and then very quietly lay the receiver on the kitchen table and leave it there while she went on with her work. From time to time she picked up the instrument, said, "Yes, I see," and laid it down again. When a prolonged silence came, she said, "Thank you for ringing," and rang off.

The weather improved, and one morning she took the children's playpen out to a small, paved yard at the side of the house. It was roofed, but it was open on one side and gave the children a view of the garden. She put down a large groundsheet and a travelling rug and left them to amuse themselves.

She saw that Randall, impressed or irritated by his sister's success in walking several paces without collapsing, had begun to pull himself upright and, with the aid of the wooden rail of the playpen, advance a step or two. Soon, she told them, they would be able to have races.

"And then," she promised, "you'll both get a great — big — prize."

She turned to go into the house and, to her surprise, heard an amused laugh. The sound came from the other side of the thick hedge that separated Julian's house from Mrs. Wray's. She heard herself addressed.

"Do come round to the gate, won't you? I've been looking at you and the babies through a tiny opening, and when you mentioned prizes, they looked so expectant that I had to laugh."

Natalie walked to the gate and into the road. From the low wooden gate next door a grey-haired woman advanced to meet her.

"We're not strangers," she said. "You're Miss Travers, and you've come to look after your brother and the twins."

"Not my brother. Only the twins," Natalie corrected. "You're Mrs. Wray."

"Nobody has as yet got round to uttering it. I was Miss Downing for far too many years for people to be able to change. Please do come into the house — can you, just for a few minutes? Or don't you care to leave the children?"

"They'll be safe for a time," Natalie said.

She followed the other woman past the small car parked at the gate and along the narrow path she had seen from her bedroom window. As they went, she assembled her impressions: thin, up-right, neat dress; hair in a neat bun, clear skin; mild grey eyes in a plain, sensible face. Large feet in low-heeled shoes, bony, work-roughened hands and a quiet, musical voice.

Mrs. Wray paused at the front door.

"A number of people came to see the house," she said, "but you're my first real visitor — that's

55

to say, the first stranger, or may I say the first friend who isn't here out of mere curiosity."

"You feel I should be carried across the threshold?"

Mrs. Wray laughed.

"No. I'm only trying to convey my pride at having a house of my own to show off. Do come in. As you see, I'm still unpacking. I did my husband's things first, in case he came a day or two early. I wanted him to feel at home at once. You know he isn't here yet?"

"No, I didn't know."

"I thought it would be better for me to come ahead and be here when the heavy luggage arrived."

Natalie was looking round. From a small, square hall, doors stood open to a long, narrow living room and two bedrooms. The rooms were neat and well furnished. Books were aligned on shelves. The floors were of polished wood, the curtains and chair covers of pale, softly blended colours.

"I've left my bedroom for later. Here" — Mrs. Wray led the way — "is my husband's. He can rearrange his things when he arrives, but I've put them, for the moment, where I thought he'd like them to be."

A man's room. Natalie saw suits hanging in the wardrobe, shoes in a row, an open drawer with piles of shirts, ties hanging from a rod. This, she realized, was the room that she could see from her bedroom window. Looking out of this one, she was surprised to see no sign of Julian's house; then she remembered that she had been looking downward through an aperture which would give no view in return.

Mrs. Wray was moving about the room, making small adjustments.

"I put the desk under that window," she said. "My husband has a lot of writing to do. He retired about two years ago — he was an inspector of schools — but he's always being asked to help with reports or to go round filling in for anybody who's ill. It means that he has to do a good deal of travelling. I do hope you'll meet him soon. You won't be leaving Downing yet, will you?"

"From where I stand," Natalie answered, "it looks as though I won't be leaving at all. As my brother agreed, it means finding a cook, a nurse and a housekeeper."

Mrs. Wray looked sympathetic.

"It's a difficult situation for you. I wish I could help in some way. I can't think of anybody who could take over from you, but I can certainly baby-sit or go in and watch the children while you shop or go to the hairdresser. I could even take them out in their pram." She was leading the way back to the hall. "I ought to invite you to meet some of my friends, but the truth is I haven't many. My sisters had friends in the town, but I seldom went out. Now I'm afraid we've quarrelled."

Natalie was looking at the neat piles of linen

placed on chairs to await sorting. She went forward and examined the embroidery on a hand towel.

"Your work?" she asked.

"Yes."

"It's beautiful."

"My sole gift," Mrs. Wray said, smiling. "It was a godsend while my father was ill. He used to like me to sit with him at times, but he didn't like being talked to or read to. So I did my embroidery until he fell asleep, and then I crept away to the kitchen and got on with work of a different kind."

They walked slowly to the gate.

"Please do come and visit me whenever you can find time." Mrs. Wray's tone was one of genuine appeal. She opened the gate, and as she did so, a car drove up and stopped. She gave an exclamation of pleasure. "Henry! How nice to see you."

Natalie looked at the driver with interest. The man with the golf clubs. The man with a key to the golf course, Henry Downing.

His eyes rested on her for a moment.

"The children well?" he inquired.

"Thank you, yes."

"Oh, have you two met?" Mrs. Wray asked in surprise.

"Only in passing, as it were," he answered. "Charming children, especially the little girl. Aunt Blanche, I can't stop. I just came to tell you that I've sent Clarice and Geraldine's furniture

58

down to their hotel cottage."

Mrs. Wray looked at him in bewilderment.

"But those cottages are already furnished," she said. "They were going to store their furniture."

"They were. But they discovered that they couldn't live with fumed oak, so they arranged to have all the hotel furniture taken out and their own put in."

"I see. Are they . . . are they happy?"

"Very. They can have their meals at the hotel, and the hotel servants do all their housework. What I came for was to ask you to drive yourself up to the house sometime today, to see if there's anything more you want to take out of it."

"I took everything that was mine."

"You took a good deal less than Clarice and Geraldine. What about carpets, curtains, pictures?"

"Thank you, Henry — but I haven't room in this house for anything more. Have you arranged for the rest of the furniture to go into store?"

"Not yet."

"Have you put the house up for sale?"

"No. Are you sure you don't want anything more out of it?"

"Quite sure. Couldn't you come inside for just a few minutes?"

"Sorry. I'm on my way to the school." He jerked his head towards the back of the car. "A load of stuff from Leo's mother. I told her she wasn't to send him food, but about a crateful arrived, sent off before he even left home. I'm going to hand it over to the headmaster for general distribution. Will you be in this evening?"

"Yes."

"Then I might drop in."

He gave Natalie a nod, raised a hand in farewell to his aunt and was gone. Mrs. Wray spoke apologetically.

"I'm sorry about that. Henry isn't usually so abrupt — it wasn't at all his usual manner. He's been rather moody ever since he arrived in England — the house has been on his mind. The idea was to sell it when my sisters and I moved out, but I think he's finding it a more difficult decision than he anticipated. The Leo he mentioned is his half-brother; he brought him over from Italy and put him into Downinghurst. I wish he'd consider coming back to England for good, but of course, there's nothing for him here."

"There's the ancestral mansion," Natalie pointed out lightly. "And his half-brother. And his aunts."

Mrs. Wray smiled.

"His half-brother will probably settle down better if he's left to himself. His aunts . . . well, we were always too old for him to make much contact. As for the ancestral mansion, he couldn't really live in it as it is. Not live with any comfort, that is. It's centuries out of date. My father was very bitter about my brother's decision to live permanently in Italy after his first

60

wife died; he felt that nobody would want to take over the house in the future, and so he refused to do anything to modernize it. It was kept in good repair, but it was never made comfortable by today's standards. Henry was born in it, but he was only twelve when his mother died and his father took him to Italy. He was at school here, but he spent all his holidays in Italy, as Leo will do. Leo's mother was very much against his coming to England, but Henry insisted."

"Why did he insist on Leo coming to school here if it wasn't with the idea of forming some after-school ties?"

"Perhaps Leo will — though I doubt it. I've seen very little of him, but I thought him rather un-English. I think what Henry wanted was to give him a sense of . . . well, of continuity. The Downings have never achieved anything that could go into the history books, but they've lived here for a very long time. They once owned the land on which the town was built. So Leo's roots are here."

"But he wasn't born here."

"Yes, he was. My brother wanted him to be born at Downing, so he and his Italian wife came over, and Leo was born at Downing House. His mother . . . I made her rooms as warm and comfortable as I could, but she hated this country, hated the climate, hated my two sisters and had very little liking for my father. As soon as she could travel, she left — she and my brother and the baby."

"Vowing never to return?"

"Yes. When my brother died, his body was brought to England and buried in the cemetery here, beside countless other Downings. But his wife — his widow — didn't come. I'm afraid you must find this family history boring."

"No, I don't. I like hearing it."

"You'll probably hear some gossip in the town about the quarrel between my sisters and myself. We were never very close — either in age or in interests. We were rather a strung-out family. There was only a year between my sisters, but it was six years before Henry's father was born, and another five before I arrived. I suppose there was family life of a kind when we were young, but when the war came, my brother served in Italy and my sisters went into Downing every day to do war work. I was left with my parents. There were servants in those days, but one by one, they vanished, until there was only one old man left. When he told me that he was going to retire, I decided that I'd done my share of looking after other people. So I installed myself here, and now I've got a husband and a home of my own, and I'm very comfortable and happy. But my sisters looked on it as desertion."

Natalie walked home thoughtfully. She felt she could now understand Henry Downing's preoccupation on the occasion of their first meeting. It couldn't be an easy decision — to let a house go after having owned it for more than three hundred years.

She reached the playpen, retrieved a ball and two toys that had been thrown over the rail and instituted a game of brick building before going indoors to prepare the midday meal.

Julian came home late that evening. He unloaded onto the kitchen table two aluminum-foil dishes containing meat and vegetables and listened to Natalie's account of her meeting with Mrs. Wray.

"I ought to have looked in to see her," he said. "No news of when her husband's arriving?"

"Soon, I gathered."

"Did the subject of Downing House come up while she was talking to her nephew?"

"She asked him if it had been put up for sale, and he said no."

"Did he say what was holding him up?"

"No. But Mrs. Wray said the house was out of date."

"We know that. If the golf club funds run to buying it, doing a bit of modernizing isn't going to present any difficulties; the membership includes an army of workmen who've offered to work at weekends — free."

"It's a pity the house has to be sold."

"Why a pity? The Downings don't want it anymore, and the golfers do. Oh, by the way, did you happen to come across those lecture notes I was working on?"

"There were only two pages. I put them in your study. Why do you call it your study if you don't work in it?"

"It was too small to take the piano and leave enough space to move round in. I go in there if I want to be quiet."

"Do you think Mrs. Wray would like to come with me to the lecture?"

"You've decided to go?"

"Yes, if the headmaster doesn't forget to send the assistant matron he talked about."

"I'll give him a reminder, if you like."

"No. If he remembers, he remembers. Go and say good night to the twins and have your shower and don't be too long, I'm hungry."

She put the food into the oven to warm and then laid two places at the table in the drawing room. She had refused to eat in the kitchen in the evenings; she had her lunch there and she fed the twins there, but she did not want to have her dinner there. She had turned the dining room into a playroom for the twins to use on inclement days, and ate dinner with Julian in the drawing room.

"I may be imagining it," Julian said over coffee, "but I thought the twins had more colour in their cheeks tonight."

"Colder weather."

"Perhaps. Did you notice a letter from their mother in my mail this morning?"

"No. I've never seen her handwriting. Any news?"

"Not much. She asked for money. I sent her a check. I suppose I've got to go on supporting her — for a time anyhow. She's got back her old job

— secretary to some MP or other."

"Where's she living?"

"With the woman she shared a room with before she met me. In other words, she's taken up the threads again. A husband and twins were just an interlude, an experiment that didn't come off. She signed the letter with her maiden name."

He said no more on the subject. After a pause Natalie asked him if his day had gone well.

"So-so," he answered. "I had young Leo Downing in for an interview this afternoon."

"Is he settling down?"

"I wouldn't know; that's not my province. You'd have to ask his housemaster and his matron about the settling-down. All I'm concerned with is music. He was sent to me because the choirmaster says he's got an exceptionally good voice but refuses to join the choir."

"Does he have to?"

"He doesn't *have* to. But if his voice is good, which it is, and if he's musical, which he is, he ought to want to."

"Did you make him want to?"

"I used tact. I began with a rather subtle approach and crept up, so to speak, on his flank. I left him for a time in doubt as to what my stand was on the matter."

"So is he in the choir or not in the choir?"

"For the moment, not."

"All that subtle approach and flank-creeping for nothing?"

"I don't see why you think it's amusing."

"Such big guns on such a small boy. Do you ever invite any of the pupils to join you in the organ loft?"

"No."

"You should invite this Leo for a Sunday or two. Tell him he can help you with your sheets of music. As it's a privilege seldom or never accorded, it'll raise him high in the estimation of the little boys fluting away in the choir stalls. When you ask him, eventually, if he cares to join them, it'll be a matter of stepping down from the organ loft to the choir stalls, not a mere matter of a new boy being shoved in."

"It's a pity you weren't at the interview."

"What's he like?"

"Self-possessed. Talking down to him is a big mistake. He aired his views on some of the masters; I was so interested that for a time I forgot to shut him up. . . . Is there any more coffee?"

"Yes. Bring it in, will you?"

He fetched it from the kitchen and poured it out.

"Anything on television for you to look at?" he asked when they had finished. "I've got to go into town to see a fellow."

She said nothing for some moments, being occupied in giving Freddie full marks for prescience.

"I think I'll do some mending," she said at last.

"Has Mrs. Gilling turned up anything yet?"

"No."

66

"Well, we'll just have to wait and hope." He was in the hall, putting on his coat. "Don't wait up for me."

The door banged, and she settled down to sew. When she went up to bed, she found the twins on their stomachs, knees drawn up, faces half buried in their pillows. She turned them over, tucked them in and then went into her room and stood for some time at the window, looking out. The night was clear, and a strong wind shook the trees that bordered the fields. She did not miss the hum of traffic that she was used to hearing at home, but she found herself listening for the surge of the sea that had been within sight and sound all her life.

The house next door was in darkness except for a light that shone from the hall onto the flagged path. At the gate she could see Henry Downing's car parked behind his aunt's. She pictured the two people in the house: the quiet woman who gave an impression of contentment, the man impatient to finish his business in Downing and depart.

She took the twins for a walk next morning. The telephone was ringing when she got back to the house, but she let it ring for a time, until she remembered that Mrs. Gilling had already telephoned her morning report. Picking up the receiver, she heard a woman's voice.

"Miss Travers?"

"Yes."

"I'm speaking from Downinghurst. I'm the

headmaster's secretary. He has asked me to confirm that you're coming to Mr. Travers's lecture on Thursday."

"I'd like to, but —"

"He says he'll send Miss Drew to look after the children. She's a trained children's nurse, so you can leave them without worrying. Will you come to the lecture?"

"Yes."

"Good. There's just one other thing. Mrs. Whitestone is inviting a few people to stay on to supper after the lecture that would, of course, include you and your brother. But it would mean Miss Drew missing dinner at the school, so —"

"I'll leave dinner here for her."

"Thank you. I'll tell her."

"How will she get here?"

"She'll go on her bicycle. I look forward to seeing you."

"Please thank Mr. Whitestone."

"I will. Good-bye."

Natalie retailed this news to Julian when he came home.

"What's Miss Drew like?" she asked.

"No idea. I'm not in touch with the school matrons. How is this one getting here?"

"Bike. I'm going to walk next door after dinner to ask Mrs. Wray if she'd like to go with me to your lecture. Do you want to come with me?"

"No. Tell her I'm busy selecting the music. If she does go with you, old Whitestone will be pleased."

"I know. He likes her."

"That's not why he'll be pleased. If she goes, Clarice and Geraldine will keep away. He had to send them an invitation — now that they're living in town, they're being accorded leading-citizen status. But they've declared war on Blanche, so where she goes, they won't go."

"Which makes it easy for anybody who doesn't want them. What kind of war?"

"Verbal. At the moment they're hinting that she's been married for her money and that her husband is coming here to live on her. . . . You had a big mail this morning. Your boyfriends getting restless?"

"No. That letter you were telling me about, from your wife — did she mention the twins?"

"No. An unnecessary question."

"Why unnecessary?" She looked at him in surprise. "She's their mother, and —"

"Look." He spoke irritably. "If a woman can do what she did — walk out and leave two infants without so much as a backward glance to see if they're being looked after — doesn't that prove that she's been able to clear them right out of her mind?"

"But it's . . . it's unnatural. It's —"

"Quite. Or not quite. Animals vary, don't they? Some of them tend their young and some of them eat their young and some of them just walk off and leave their young. She was the walking-off kind. One of the masters referred to her as my ex-wife. I pointed out that she wasn't, yet,

69

so he said he'd refer to her in future as the dear departed. He thought that was funny. I didn't. Is that dinner warmed up yet? If so, let's eat."

There was a light outside Mrs. Wray's house when Natalie walked next door after dinner. Mrs. Wray, answering her knock, looked delighted to see her.

"How nice! Please come in." She drew Natalie in and closed the door. "I thought you were Henry — he promised to come and have a late dinner with me. You've had yours?"

"Yes. I can't stay a moment. I just came to ask you if —"

She stopped. She was being urged gently but firmly into the living room.

"You've had dinner, the babies are no doubt in bed and your brother is there to see to them if they need anything. So you can spare me ten minutes. I nearly telephoned to ask you and your brother to come over for drinks, to meet my husband — he came this afternoon. But unfortunately he had to go back to London to see somebody. Now sit there and tell me whether you'd like anything to drink."

"No, thank you. What I came to ask was whether you'd like to go with me to the school lecture. My brother's going to —"

"I know exactly what he's going to do. I took Leo out, and he told me every detail — very indignantly. It appears that the juniors are not going to the lecture. He wanted me to lodge a protest with the headmaster. I suppose it's the

70

kind of thing his mother would have done at the school he went to in Florence, but I had to explain that I couldn't do it here. It isn't that he expects special treatment — it's just that he's always been given anything he asked for. He — Oh, why don't you stay?"

It was such a forlorn plea that Natalie almost sat down again.

"I'd like to stay," she said, "but it's begun to rain."

"And all you've got to protect you is that light jacket. Then you must go."

"Will you come to the lecture?"

"I'd love to. Shall I walk over to you, or as you'll have to pass my gate, perhaps it would be better if you stopped and sounded the horn? I'll be quite ready."

Natalie said good-bye and, putting her head down against the heavy drops of rain, walked to the gate. As she reached it, Henry Downing's car drew up. The rain was now coming down heavily. He got out and held the gate open for her.

"Natalie, hurry — you'll be soaked," Mrs. Wray called.

"You can't walk in this downpour," Henry said. "Get in and I'll drive you home."

"No, thank you. I only —"

"Look, I insist," he broke in. He had opened the car door. "Get in, will you? Get in before we're both soaked."

She got in. He raised a hand to Mrs. Wray and then took his place at the wheel.

"Direct me, will you?"

"Second left, first right and then straight on," she said.

He drove a short distance and then stopped the car and turned to her with a frown.

"There's no right turning off this lane," he pointed out.

"I'm so sorry; I never did know my right from my left. Try second left and then straight on and let's see where that gets us."

"What's the name of the road you live in?"

"Highcliff Walk."

"Highcliff . . . Look, is this a joke?"

"No. You insisted on taking me home, and you asked for directions. I'm doing my best."

"Where do you live?"

"Fourteen Highcliff Walk, Brighton, Sussex. I've forgotten the code number. It won't take you more than four hours to run me there. Maybe five."

There was a pause.

"All right. I apologize," he said.

"Forget it."

"Where do you live when you're not living at Fourteen Highcliff Walk, Brighton, Sussex?"

"With my brother, Julian Travers, next door to your aunt."

"She told me you were Travers's sister. I forgot he lived next door. The two children?"

"His. Twins. Rowena and Randall. I'm in temporary charge — and it's time I got back to them."

He turned the car, drove back and stopped outside Julian's gate. Rain was still falling heavily, but before he could get out, she had opened the door on her side and was running up the steps to the front door.

"Thanks for the lift," she called over her shoulder.

She heard him laugh and carried the sound indoors with her. There was not enough laughter in Julian's house.

Julian was on his way up to bed.

"Is she coming to the lecture?" he asked.

"Yes."

"Remind me to tell old Whitestone, will you? Good night."

She did some clearing-up and then put out the lights and went up to bed. Looking out of the window into the darkness, she saw the light shining on the flagged path — and at the gate, rain-washed and gleaming, Henry Downing's car.

He wanted to get away from Downing, but something was keeping him here. That, she thought, made two of them.

Chapter

4

On the evening of the lecture, Miss Drew arrived punctually, pedalling into the drive on a bicycle with sunken handlebars and a profusion of gears. She was standing beside it when Natalie opened the door, and one of the drawbacks the head-master had mentioned became apparent in the terse, brusque manner of her greeting.

" 'Evening. The name's Drew. Got orders to take over while you're out — that is, if you're Miss Travers."

"I am. It's nice of you to come. Would you like to put your bike into the garage?"

"Nope. Where I'd like it is in the hall. No need to worry about mud; the tires are dry."

She was carrying the bicycle up the steps as she spoke. She looked about twenty. She was of middle height, with a broad frame, a long face, a long nose, narrow grey eyes and jutting chin. Her hair, soft and close-cropped and curly, seemed unsuited to the purposeful features below.

"Oh, you've got a pram littering the place," she said. "Never mind; I can shove it aside. Take that end, will you? That's it. Can't leave the bike outside; I've had two looted out of so-called lockup garages, and I didn't get enough out of

74

the insurance to make it worthwhile losing a third." She took off her short leather coat and hung it up. "Where are these twins I've come to look after?"

"In here, having their supper." Natalie led the way into the kitchen. "Randall and Rowena."

Miss Drew studied them with a gaze that was at first keenly professional but, to Natalie's relief, softened to an expression approaching tenderness.

"Well, now." She leaned her hands on the table and addressed the two silent, staring children. "I like you. You'll like me, too, when you get over the first shock. I'm going to be married soon, to a nice, solid chap down in Devon, and we're going to have sets of twins just like you." She straightened and faced Natalie. "Children! All my life, kids, kids, kids. Eight of them in our family, and I'm the eldest, so you can imagine. It's a good thing I'm fond of them, or I would've got hold of a rolling pin long ago and knocked a few of 'em on the head. Now you can take me on a quick tour and show me where all the kids' things are kept. What's that hanging on the door — their diet sheet?"

"Yes."

Miss Drew examined it.

"Needs revising," she said. "The quantities'll have to be increased. I'll bring it up to date when I've got them into bed."

"Thank you. Will you come upstairs?"

"They're in good condition," Miss Drew conceded on the way up, "but you need to watch out for changes of diet. It takes a bit of time for deficiencies to show. From what I've heard, Mr. Travers's wife didn't take much interest in them. The nurse at the surgery told me she didn't know the first thing about child rearing, so maybe the kids'll be better off without her. I bet Mr. Travers was pleased to see you. What are you going to do — live here with him?"

"No."

"Then what? I didn't see a queue of nannies outside the house, waiting to sign on. It's time this town had a day nursery — if there'd been one, your brother could've left the twins there during the day when his wife went off. Nice bathroom. This the only one?"

"No. My brother's room has one."

"This the nursery? I'm glad it's a double cot. Some people don't like them, but I do. Do the kids go straight to sleep, or do you tell them a story?"

"I just put them to bed and go away and leave the little blue bulb switched on. Randall tells the story."

"Like our Maureen. She's the baby. She's not two yet, but she gabbles nonstop. Now let's go down, and I'll see them through the rest of their supper. Don't you bother about me — I'll find my way around."

"I made you a small steak-and-kidney pie and some baked apples for your dinner," Natalie said when they were back in the kitchen. "I hope you like them."

76

"I'll eat anything. Always could, all my life. Mum says I take a lot of filling. Water with a squeeze of lemon's what I like to drink."

Natalie brought out a lemon and the lemon squeezer.

"And if I fancy a bit of cheese, with a biscuit, maybe, could I —"

"In here." Natalie displayed cheese, butter and biscuits. "Please help yourself to anything you need."

"I will. Now you can forget about me. I've never met kids who didn't get on with me, and these two won't be any different."

Natalie paused on her way to the door.

"Did you mean what you said about getting married soon?"

"End of next term. I don't wear a ring because I haven't got one. The squire said they were a waste of dough, and I agreed. He's solid, like I said, and he lives in Devon, close to where our house is, but he's not a squire, only that's what we've always called him. He's a farmer. I could have had him or his brother, like Queen Victoria. I dunno why Victoria chose Albert, but I chose Ken because he's the one who's going to inherit the house, and I want a house. None of that moving in with the in-laws, thank you very much."

"If you want to look at television, it's in the dining room."

"Which is that?" Miss Drew opened the door and inspected it. "I like this better than the other room. Not so cluttered. But I shan't be looking at the telly; I like to keep my ears for listening to the kids. We don't go much for the telly in our family, only the younger ones. The older ones are always out, and my mum can't sit settled for long, and my dad gets behind the evening paper and stays there. And as the squire says, they don't miss much. He can't be bothered with it either — he says half of it's corn and the other half's porn. I've got behind with my letter to him — d'you mind if I sit in here and write?"

"Please do."

Natalie left the house, drove next door and found Mrs. Wray at the gate.

"I heard you start the car, so I came out," she said. "Who's with the twins?"

"One of the assistant matrons from the school, sent by the headmaster. Miss Drew."

"Nice?"

"Breezy. She's used to children — she's got seven brothers and sisters. You'll have to direct me to the school."

"When you say 'school,' you have to specify. I think there are ten different buildings in all. And no bicycles allowed, for getting from one to the other."

"Do you often go to school functions?"

"Hardly ever. In fact, I hardly went anywhere — but I did try to pay an occasional visit to the Whitestones; they're my oldest friends. I was beginning to fear they might leave Downing when he retired, but I'm glad to know they've decided to stay somewhere near. I don't suppose he could really settle in any other part of the country after his forty years at the school. He's very fond of your brother. He admits he was worried on their first meeting — your brother has a rather abstracted manner. But look what he's done for the music of the school! I'm looking forward to hearing him speak this evening. I hoped Henry would come, but he said he couldn't manage it. I think he wants to get through all his business here so that he can get away."

"Back to Italy?"

"Yes. But he still seems to be in two minds about whether to sell the house or not. You turn right at the crossroads."

When they reached the Music Department, they were received by a senior master, passed to a junior master and thence to a prefect, who led them to the concert hall and showed them to their seats. Watching the school file in, Natalie was surprised to find that she was feeling nervous. It was the first time she had heard Julian speak in public, and she remembered with some misgiving the scanty lecture notes he had scribbled. If he had been at the piano, if he had been playing the flute . . . those were his instruments, and she knew that he could hold any audience. Speaking was something else.

He was given a round of applause when he came onto the platform, but in the succeeding moments she felt again that he was ill-prepared, for he advanced to the front and then stood as though waiting for his cue. Then he began to speak.

"Good evening. I called this lecture Interpretation because I couldn't think of a better word. But it needs amplifying.

"We all know that a playwright writes plays. Some playwrights — Shakespeare, for example — wrote great plays, with great parts that are acted again and again by great actors. Each actor gives his own interpretation of the part, and you will in time be able to criticize each interpretation and agree with it — or disagree with it.

"A composer writes music. This evening I am going to play excerpts from the recordings of some of the greatest music played by the greatest orchestras under the greatest conductors. I hope to be able to show you that each conductor gives the work an interpretation as individual, as clearly stamped with his image, as — shall we say? — a series of actors playing Hamlet."

The coughing had ceased; the shuffling had subsided. Natalie relaxed.

The headmaster, having assured himself that the interest of the audience had been caught, gave his mind to the assistant masters seated at the end of the rows occupied by their pupils. All of them, he noted without surprise, divided their attention between the lecturer and the lecturer's sister. Well, she was a beauty, and he would have been suspicious of any young fellow who didn't show his appreciation, in however guarded a manner. Perhaps she wasn't beautiful; perhaps she only gave the impression of beauty. Skin . . . well, his wife's had been like that, once. Lovely slender neck — he didn't suppose those young fellows were looking at her neck. Large eyes, beautifully set, blue but not wishy-washy blue. And a mouth . . . come to think of it, how rarely you saw a really beautiful mouth like hers. Good manners, that girl had, or perhaps it was a good manner. Unconscious of the male interest she roused? Couldn't be. Unresponsive? Hard to tell. She certainly took it in her stride.

He sighed. Pity he couldn't shave a couple of decades off his age and feel his blood quickening again. Those were good days, when you could eat prime underdone beef and drink your fill of port and tuck away the butter and Brie and keep cholesterol out of the conversation. All over. All gone forever. Now you had to live on sunflower seeds. A woman would have to suck a lot of cider through a number of straws before his pulse quickened. And speaking of cider, what sort of impression would that young Devonshire matron make on the Travers household? It wasn't the first time he had found her something to do outside the school, but she didn't seem to have the knack of making adults take to her. Children, yes. Well, one would have to wait and see.

When the lecture was over, Mrs. Whitestone led the supper guests into a large room in which a number of small tables had been spread with food and drink.

"Plates and knives and forks over here. Will you all help yourselves, please?"

It was a large and varied meal. Mrs. Whitestone told Natalie that she could claim no credit.

"About four years ago," she explained, "we closed the school kitchen and brought in a firm of caterers. It's been a great success. The only thing I have to watch is the amount of fried food they serve."

Natalie was enjoying herself. Most of those present belonged to the school — senior and junior masters, two secretaries, the head girl and head boy. At the end of the room two young pianists at two pianos played light background music. The masters circulated with wine. The time passed so swiftly that she was surprised when Julian came up to her and told her that it was time to go.

Before she left, the headmaster took her aside.

"You remember I spoke to you about a bit of coaching?" he asked.

"Yes. I hoped —"

"You hoped it wouldn't come to pass. But it has. I'm not asking you to do it for long. I've usually been able to arrange coaching in the school or in the town, but the new intake this term has caused problems. Two fourteen-year-olds from Malaysia want their English brushed up — there's not much to brush — but I've fixed that. I've also found someone to take the maths group. What I'd like you to do, if you will — remember that this is a business arrangement —

is to coach a couple of teenage girls in history, Thirty Years War — and I'd like to send young Leo Downing to you. He doesn't need coaching in the ordinary sense; what he does need is someone to tell him a few Bible stories."

"Bible stories?"

"His classmates discovered that he'd never heard of any of the Bible characters that most children in this country, even in this irreligious age, grow up with. Cain and Abel, for example. Joseph and his chromatic coat. Moses in the bulrushes. It began when the Scripture master asked them to explain the term 'corn in Egypt.' None of them knew, but in the subsequent discussion a few more biblical allusions came up, and the depth of young Downing's ignorance was revealed. Asked about the Ark, he said it was a rainbow in the sky. Will you see if you can fill in some of the blanks?"

"I'll do my best."

"Monday?"

"Yes."

"I'll send you the history couple first, two to three, and Leo'll follow them, three to four. Thank you; that's a load off my mind."

Julian took Mrs. Wray home in his car. Natalie drove alone and arrived to find Miss Drew putting on her leather jacket and tying a scarf round her head.

"Have a good time?" she inquired.

"Yes. Thank you so much for —"

"Enjoyed myself. Not a peep out of the twins

after I'd tucked them in. I had my dinner — I topped it up with a bit of cheese, hope you don't mind — and then I sat at that dining table and got through four long letters. Look here, I've got a suggestion: I haven't got many friends round here, and sometimes — 'specially now, when the weather's beginning to turn nasty — I'm at a loose end on my afternoons off. If it's all right by you, I could pop in here and take over."

Natalie hesitated.

"Wouldn't that be rather a busman's holiday?"

"A what? Oh, I see what you mean. No, it wouldn't, not really. If you didn't want me, you could always put me off. But I like that room, nice and quiet, and I get on with the twins, so you could go out and forget them. I don't have to be back at the school till late."

"You're very kind, but —"

"Don't decide now. Think it over. And don't forget to follow that chart I left. If you'll hold the door open, I'll get my bike out."

When she got onto the bicycle in the drive, she had to swerve to avoid Julian's car, which missed her by inches. She shouted something at him; Natalie could not catch the words, but they sounded uncomplimentary. Julian, coming in and locking the front door, said angrily that it had not been his fault.

"That's a racing bike," he pointed out. "She went out of the gate like the Tour de France."

He went on to explain that the reason for his offer to take Mrs. Wray home had been the hope

84

of finding out from her how long it would be before her nephew, Henry Downing, put his house up for sale. It was empty; the occupants had removed themselves; a firm of auctioneers was said to be waiting to remove the remaining effects to their sale room.

"So what's the holdup? Downing's still hanging round the town — why doesn't he get things moving?"

"Didn't Mrs. Wray know?"

"No. All she said — very helpful, I must say — was that as far as she knew, there was nothing to stop him from selling. She said she'd be sorry to see the house sold — that's natural enough — and she also admitted that the place was out of date." He gave a prolonged yawn. "I'm going to get myself something to eat."

"Eat? I saw your plate at supper — piled as high as Everest."

"Lecturing's hungry work."

She followed him into the kitchen. He was rummaging in a cupboard.

"Where's the cheese?" he asked.

"In there."

"I can't see it. You look."

Natalie looked, in that cupboard and then in several others.

"We didn't eat it," Julian said. "There was a big hunk left. And there was a packet of biscuits. I'll start on those."

"I can't find them either. Perhaps Miss Drew ate them."

"I thought you said you left dinner for her."

"I did. I made her a steak-and-kidney pie and some baked apples."

He looked at the plates and dishes that had been washed and left to drain.

"Was that the dish you made the pie in?"

"Yes."

"If she got through that, she didn't need a pound of cheese and a packet of biscuits, did she? Let's have another look for them. Or wait . . ."

He walked to the refuse bin and pressed the pedal. The lid sprang up to reveal the cheese wrapping, the crumpled biscuit packet, two empty sardine tins, an empty can of celery soup and a small empty can of baked beans.

He raised his head and gazed speechlessly at Natalie. Then he spoke in an enraged tone.

"She didn't get through that lot by herself. She obviously invited someone in for a nice little picnic — one of her boyfriends. I'll have a few words with the headmaster in the morning."

"You can't do that, Julian. In the first place, I don't think she invited anybody. She's got a fiancé in Devon, and she spent the evening writing to him. She must have been hungry."

"Hungry? *Hungry?* She —"

"And if she did eat too much, you can't say so. She came on the understanding that she'd get her dinner here, and you can't make a fuss about the size of it. She's just got a good appetite, that's all. What are you doing?"

86

"Looking to see how much she took away."

"Don't be idiotic."

"She doesn't like the school food, that's what it is. So when she gets a chance, she stocks up. What's the betting she won't decide that we're cheaper than a café and offer to come and twin-sit on her days off?" He saw the look that flitted across Natalie's face and spoke in a tone of suspicion. "You're not planning to let her in again, are you?"

"Will you find someone else to come in? No, you won't. What does it matter how much she ate?"

"Count it up in money: that cheese, best you can buy. Expensive biscuits. Soup, beans, sardines, steak, kidneys, apples, gas to cook . . . how about bread?" He peered into the bread bin. "My God, not a crumb! What do I do for toast in the morning? She didn't finish off the milk, too, did she?"

"There's enough for the twins."

"I see. The twins have their cereal, but I don't get my coffee unless I drink it black."

"Yes, you do. If you can go a bit later in the morning, the milk will be delivered."

He said nothing beyond three words that summed up his opinion of Miss Drew. Then he poured out some brandy for himself, added a dash of water and took it upstairs to bed.

Chapter

5

Monday afternoon brought the school car and two girls aged fourteen and fifteen dressed in the school uniform of navy blue skirts and blazers. The chauffeur's only concession to uniform was a peaked cap bearing the name of the school.

"I'll be back for this lot," he told Natalie, "and I'll bring the young gent."

"Thank you."

She led the girls into the dining room, and they took their places at the long table. There was a good deal of giggling during the preliminaries, the older girl announcing that she hated history and didn't know Charles the Bold from Charles the Bald. It took Natalie five minutes to deflate the pair and a further ten to convince them that they were there to learn, whether they wanted to or not. The remainder of the hour was peaceful and produced results so gratifying that the arrival of the school car came as an unwelcome interruption.

The historians departed; Natalie ushered in Leo Downing, altering, as she did so, the mental sketch she had made of him. She had expected, perhaps from the headmaster's tone when speaking of him, a sophisticated, if not precocious, schoolboy. He seemed to her now, however, to be no different from his fellows except in appearance — he looked like every little Italian boy to be seen in every Italian city: olive-skinned, with large, long-lashed brown eyes and thick, wavy brown hair. His manner was composed. As he took his place at the table, his gaze went slowly round the room, missing nothing, and although his face was expressionless, she received the distinct impression that he found the decor sub-standard.

"I am here to know about the Bible," he explained. "I don't see why I should learn about it, but when the names of the people are mentioned and I haven't heard about them, the other boys laugh. I could laugh at them for a lot of things, but I don't, because it isn't polite. And I don't mind if they laugh at me, so why should I come here?"

"Simply to gain a bit more knowledge. Are you a Catholic?"

"If I am anything, yes. But my mother doesn't believe in God. She says that there are many, and everybody should make up their minds for themselves. Do you believe in any?"

"Well, yes, I do. One, anyway. But what you're here for is to widen your general knowledge by being able to recognize names that most people, in some cases people of other religions, too, recognize. Like Abraham and —"

"Who?"

"Abraham was the founder of the Jewish nation. The Hebrew nation."

"Is it interesting to know about him?"

"Some people think so. He lived about two thousand three hundred years before Christ, and —"

"How many?"

"About two thousand three hundred. He had a wife named Sarah, and they had a son named Isaac. There's a story that God ordered Abraham to kill him, but —"

"Kill who?"

"His son, Isaac."

"Kill his son?"

"Yes. It was a sort of test."

"To kill his own son?"

"Yes."

"And did he kill him?"

"No. He was just going to when God stopped him."

"After telling him to do it?"

"Yes."

"God changed His mind?"

"Yes. Well, no. He just wanted to find out if Abraham trusted Him."

"Trusted him to kill his son?"

Natalie decided to retreat.

"Abraham's a bit complicated. Suppose we go on to Moses?"

"I know about Moses. He was put in a basket, I don't know why. I don't know about Joseph."

They discussed Joseph. Natalie, facing for the first time the vast scope of the Old Testament, came to the conclusion that she had undertaken this mission rather too lightly. She was not sorry to find that Leo provided some light relief by slipping facts about his own background into accounts of Esau and Jacob. As the lesson advanced, she learned some of his views on his origins.

"My mother says when I've finished being at this school, I can go home and stay there always."

"Do you think of Italy as home?"

"At present, yes. I have never lived anywhere else."

"It wasn't your father's home."

"No. He went away from here because his father was a silly old man. My mother told me that. But I don't know why my father wanted to be buried here. If he liked it so much that he wanted to come back and be buried, why did he go away? Henry — he's my half-brother — says you can live in another country and still like your own country best, but I think that's silly. He's coming to fetch me after my lesson. I forgot to tell the chauffeur not to come."

At the end of the hour only one car was waiting outside. The school car was driving away; Henry Downing was leaning against his. She was struck by the change in his manner. His pose was relaxed, his air casual, his expression faintly amused. He addressed her with friendly ease.

"Good afternoon. I came to fetch Leo. Leo, you forgot to tell the chauffeur not to come back. It's all right, Miss Travers; I'll get him back to the school."

"Thank you." She spoke again as he was getting into the car. "You'll take him straight back, won't you?"

From the driving seat he moved a hand in a series of twists, representing the curves he would have to negotiate on the way.

"More or less," he said.

"He has an appointment with my brother at half past four."

"I'll make a note."

His tone was flippant and, she thought, provocative. She decided to ignore it; she said goodbye to Leo, reminded him that the next coaching session was on Wednesday and went into the house.

She asked Julian at dinner if he had seen Leo Downing that afternoon. He looked at her in surprise.

"How did you know I was seeing him?"

"You mentioned it. Did he arrive on time?"

"He didn't arrive at all. I was told he hadn't got back from his lesson with you. If you're going to overrun your coaching time, you ought to let the school know."

On Wednesday afternoon Leo disembarked from the school car and held the door open politely for the departing history pupils. Then he told the chauffeur that he need not return.

"That all right, miss?" the man asked Natalie.

She nodded.

"Yes, quite all right."

"Henry's taking me," Leo explained, taking

92

his seat at the table. "Perhaps we'll have tea on the way back, like we did last time."

Ten minutes before the lesson was due to end, Natalie rose.

"Time to go," she said.

He looked up in surprise.

"But Henry —"

"That's all right. We'll meet him on the way."

They met him at the end of the lane. He slowed down; Natalie kept her eyes straight ahead and her foot on the accelerator.

"That was him! That was Henry!" Leo exclaimed. "We've passed him."

"He'll catch us up," said Natalie tranquilly. "I don't know that make of car he's driving — what is it?"

He was still telling her when she drew up outside the school.

When she got back to Julian's house, Henry Downing's car was standing in the drive. He walked over to open her car door.

"Not safe to leave the twins alone in the house," he said reprovingly. "Suppose there'd been a fire?"

"You would have been here to rescue them. Will you please not come to fetch Leo anymore? The school car will take him back."

"That means I have to pay extra for transport. They put it on the bill, and the bill comes to me. Just think of the waste, and not only waste of money; waste of petrol, too."

"I'd take it up with the headmaster if I were

you. Will you excuse me? I have to give the twins their tea."

"I was going to take Leo to the new teashop in town. We went there on Monday, and we were both looking forward to another feast. You've done us out of it. He'll get his tea at school, but I won't get anything. Unless you'd be so good . . ."

She had gone up the steps. She turned and looked down at him.

"I don't take sugar," he said. "And only a little milk, not enough to deprive the twins."

She could read nothing in his expression except hope.

"Your aunt would give you tea," she temporized.

"Her husband's expected. I'd be in the way."

She opened the front door.

"Come in."

"Thank you."

She took him to the kitchen, put water in the kettle and asked him to watch it while she went upstairs to fetch the twins. Julian could carry one under each arm, but she preferred to make two journeys. When Henry saw her coming down with Randall, he went up and fetched Rowena.

"Flirtatious, this one," he remarked as he unclasped her arms from round his neck and lowered her into her high chair.

"You weren't holding her properly. She felt insecure."

"I was beginning to feel insecure, too. Can I help you make the tea?"

"No, thanks. I haven't anything to give you to eat, I'm afraid."

"You weren't expecting me," he said indulgently. "But as you live next door to my favourite aunt, and as we're both trapped for a time in this town, I may — who knows? — take to dropping in at this time on Leo's lesson days. Why, incidentally, are you teaching him Scripture?"

"I'm not teaching him Scripture. The boys in his form discovered that he didn't know Adam from Eve, so the headmaster asked me to introduce him to a few of the better-known biblical characters."

"So that he'll know all that the other boys know?"

"Yes."

"Very poor psychology. Your object should be to teach him not what all the other boys know, but some things the other boys don't know."

"There are certain biblical allusions that children in this country are expected to understand."

"Lot's wife and the pillar of salt, for example. A great waste of time. The way to raise Leo in the esteem of his classmates is to break new ground, give him some facts with which he can floor the other fellows. Forget about Cain and Abel, and switch to Abidan, the son of Gideoni, or Ahiezer, the son of Ammishaddai. All the other boys will know about Balaam's ass, but will they know why Balaam was with Balak, and where they were going when the angel got in the donkey's way? No, they won't. Teach Leo about Zelophehad, whose daughters were called Mahlah, Noah, Hoglah, Milcah and Tirzah."

"Noah? Daughter?"

"That's just what the other boys will say, thinking they've caught Leo out. But this particular Noah was a daughter. Poor old Zelophehad had no sons."

"You can take this up with the headmaster, too, when you're talking to him about the transport bills."

"Will you mind if I go on dropping into tea like this?"

"I'd rather give you tea than have you encouraging Leo to break the school rules. I think that was an irresponsible thing to do, especially as both Mrs. Wray and the headmaster seem to think he might have trouble settling down."

"They're both wrong. Leo will settle down anywhere — for as long as it suits him. The moment he gets bored, he'll reach for his return ticket. Like his mother. Only she reaches for her traveller's checks. Do you like him?"

"Yes. But I don't know why you insisted on bringing him to England."

"Who says I insisted?"

"Your aunt. If he reaches for his return ticket, will you insist on his staying?"

He took the cup of tea she handed him.

"My bet is that he'll settle," he said. "He's already showing the first glimmers of interest in the fact that he was born in this town. So I'm pretty certain he'll stay. But you, my aunt told me, will depart as soon as you've found a substitute wife and mother. She said you weren't going to find that easy, and I agree with her. That's why I said we were both trapped. I've got a room at the hotel and I'm waiting, not to see if Leo settles, but to decide whether to cut or not to cut the last strands of the Downing connection in the town."

"I thought —" she began, and stopped.

"You thought?"

"I was only going to say that everyone seems to expect you to sell your house. I mean that they expected you to sell it when your aunts left it."

"That's what I expected, too."

He did not pursue the subject. He had helped himself to some of the twins' biscuits and, while eating one, was balancing the rest in an attempt to build a house. Each time it collapsed, the twins shouted with laughter.

"I'm sorry to break up this party," Natalie said after a time, "but . . ."

He put the biscuits back on the plate and rose.

"Thank you for the tea. Is there any chance of your leaving your brother in charge of the children one evening and coming out to dinner with me?"

She thought that no invitation she had ever received had been uttered in so impersonal a tone. Her own was as casual as she replied.

"There might be. But he usually goes out after dinner, to see people he didn't have time to see

97

during school hours. Thanks all the same."

He drove away. She went back thoughtfully to the twins. The telephone was ringing, but she ignored it; it would be Mrs. Gilling, and there had been enough purposeless calls from that quarter.

But when she answered a call that evening, she learned that Miss Drew had been ringing at intervals throughout the afternoon.

"Thought your phone had packed up," she said. "Just wanted to tell you that I'm going to take you up on that invitation to pop in on my free days. I've changed to Fridays, but if that's not convenient, I can change back again. Will it be all right if I show up on Friday?"

Natalie hesitated, but not for long. This was her only chance of getting away from the house for any length of time. She could not leave the twins unless someone reliable came in to look after them — and though she now knew some of Miss Drew's drawbacks, she also knew that she could be trusted to keep the children safe and happy.

"Yes, do come," she said.

"I'll bring my own tea, sandwiches and that."

"I can easily —"

"No, don't you bother. You can go off and enjoy yourself, and if you want to make a date for supper, go ahead, and I'll stay on."

To this, Natalie replied firmly that she would be back at half past six.

"See you Friday, then," Miss Drew said, and rang off.

Natalie would have liked to keep this arrangement from Julian, but found on his arrival that evening that he already knew of it. He was not pleased.

"I was waylaid by that girl, that assistant matron, forget her name," he said. "I can't think what's got into you, letting her in again."

"It was nice of her to offer to come."

"That's what you think. The fact is that she's got nowhere else to go on her free afternoons. People used to invite her when she first came to the school, but they gave up after a time because they couldn't stand her. She gets one foot in and starts running the place. You haven't offered to feed her this time, have you?"

"No. She's bringing her own tea."

"And leaving before I come home to dinner, I hope."

Natalie hoped so, too, but was only reassured when Miss Drew, bumping her bicycle up the steps on her arrival, stated that she was going to the cinema at half past six.

"Saw the posters as I went past," she explained. "I wouldn't have thought they'd have shown a film like that in a place like this. You wait, all the teenagers in town will queue up to get in, and all the old-timers will queue up to keep them out. There was the same trouble when the headmaster gave in over cohabiting."

"Over —"

Miss Drew was taking off her coat.

"Accommodation in this town's hard to find," she explained. "The arts master and the junior gym mistress were looking for somewhere to live — separately — but all there was was this one flat, so they said why not share it, so they did, and the headmaster had to make up his mind one way or the other, but he didn't take long to decide, because look at the number of visiting masters there are in the school — who knows what they get up to in their private lives? You can't stop them, can you? Like this film. If people want to go, they'll go. Wait till you see the posters. . . . The twins up yet?"

"No."

"Then I'll take over. And look, you'd better use some shopping time to top up their wardrobes. We're coming on to winter, and I looked through their stuff, and believe me, they need new outfits."

This, at the outset of her acquaintance with Miss Drew, might have surprised Natalie, but she was learning. The only surprise was that her own wardrobe, and Julian's, had not been given a similar looking-through.

"There's a shop just opened next door to Boots," Miss Drew went on. "One of those maternity-and-children's-wear places, not expensive, at least not more expensive than anywhere else. The kids need day and night wear. You know their measurements?"

"I think so."

"I'll make you a list, and then you won't leave anything out."

Natalie found the shop, worked down the list

and spent so much money that she had to add a check of her own to the money Julian had given her for expenses. An obliging salesgirl helped her carry the parcels to the parking lot, her chin pressed against the topmost to keep it from sliding to the pavement.

Her next purchases were bread, butter, jam and milk. Miss Drew had brought her tea, but there was no guarantee that she would not supplement it with anything she could find in the kitchen cupboards. The only precaution Natalie had taken was to hide Julian's favourite delicacy — a tin of French liver pâté — up in his room.

From the shopping area she drove to the garage to which Julian always took his car for servicing. But when she walked to the cubbyhole that served as office and told a gum-chewing foreman what she wanted, he shook his head.

"Full up, we are. All this week and all next. I'll put your name down. Only other chance is to have her done straight away. The chap who had this slot just rung in to say he's been in a accident, went the wrong way up a signpost, so you can be done instead. But you'll have to make up your mind quick."

"How long would the servicing take?"

"Couple of hours."

She hesitated for a moment — and then she saw Henry Downing's car draw up in the road behind her own. He walked to the petrol pump, saw her, changed direction and came to join her. He looked like a man with time on his hands and every intention of using it agreeably.

"Breakdown?" he inquired.

"If you know the lady, you could take her home," the foreman suggested. "Wants her car greased. I'll send it back with one of our chaps in a couple of hours."

"You needn't do that," Henry said. "I'll bring Miss Travers back to collect it."

"Right. That's it, then."

The foreman drove the car down to the lower regions. Henry and Natalie walked out into the street.

"Two hours," Henry said when they were in his car. "I could invite you to have tea with me, in return for the tea you gave me. Or I could take you back to your brother's house. Or I could ask you if you'd care to come up to my house; I've got to go there to see to a couple of things. Three choices. Three caskets. I suppose you had to act that scene when you were at school?"

"Yes. Doesn't every fifth form have to go through it every year?"

"I suppose you were Portia?"

"Of course. Who were you?"

"The Prince of Morocco, all blacked up." He had made no move to put the car in motion. "Do you remember what I said to you at Belmont?"

"No."

"Then I'll remind you. I said: 'Mislike me not for my complexion.' "

"There was more of it. Go on."

"I'll have to roll back the years."

The shadow'd livery of the burnish'd sun
To whom I am a neighbour and near bred.

It was a good speech, I would have been more of a success if the black paint hadn't made my face stiff and affected my diction. I wonder if old Whitestone remembers my lamentable performance, among so many other princes of Morocco he's had to sit and watch? Remember what you said to me?"

"Yes. I said:

Yourself, renowned prince, then stood as fair
As any comer I have look'd on yet
For my affection.

"And I said: 'Even for that I thank you.' A nice dignity Shakespeare showed when dealing with the mixture of races. Rather different from our present-day attitude. Well, which casket?"

"I'd like to go and see your house, but there's something I have to do first: I want to put an advertisement in the local paper. For domestic staff."

"Then we'll do it, and when it's done, I'll drive you up to the house. By advertisement, you mean notice?"

"What's the difference?"

"I can't tell you — I never worked it out. But the headmaster always stressed that you advertised only when you wanted to sell. If you wanted something, you put in a notice."

"Tell him I don't agree. A notice is Stick No Bills, or Queue Here, or No Trespassers."

"I see. So let's go and put in your advertisement."

"Not the daily paper. The one that comes out on Saturdays."

"Is this the first time you've put in a notice, that's to say, advertisement?"

"Yes. I would have put one in the daily papers, but Mrs. Gilling said it wouldn't be necessary. Mrs. Gilling, if you know who Mrs. Gilling is, promised to find someone."

"Everybody knows who Mrs. Gilling is. And Mrs. Gilling knows who everybody is, so if she fell down on the assignment, it doesn't look hopeful."

"She seems to be trying only local people. This weekly paper covers more ground, doesn't it?"

"It might reach the eyes of the unemployed in a few neighbouring villages."

"Do you know where the newspaper offices are?"

He started the car and waited for a break in the traffic before falling into line.

"I used to know," he answered. "I was born here and I lived here until I was twelve and I was at school here until I was seventeen. But each time I've been away and come back, they seem to have moved things around. How are you going to word this appeal?"

"My brother had some ideas, but he gave up. Cook-nurse-housekeeper-laundress. Imagine the rush of applicants."

"Are you combining all those functions?"

"I'm just running the house, that's all."

"You like housework?"

"No, I don't, if you mean sweeping and scrubbing. But I like living in a clean and reasonably tidy house, and you can't have one unless you do a certain amount of work in it. Julian's house is modern and it's well equipped and once I got it looking decent, it's been easy to keep it that way. But you can't expect anybody else to take it on alone."

"I suppose not. It's going to be tricky — the wording, I mean. You don't want to frighten prospective applicants."

He stopped the car outside the office of the weekly newspaper, led her inside and up to a wide counter on which were printed forms.

"Here you are." He handed her one and gave her his pen. "How about 'Help Wanted'?"

"I'd like to put 'Children's Nurse.' That's the most important function, after all."

" 'Wanted: Devoted Nanny.' "

"Not nanny. I have a feeling that any nannies that still exist would want a full staff. How about 'Woman Wanted'?"

"Why a woman? Why not a man? A man can cook and run a house."

"A man couldn't be a mother to the twins."

"All they need is affection and protection. Would you say they cared which sex wrapping those came in?"

"I don't know. Mothers are the natural —"

"Some mothers. Let's settle for children's nurse in one ad, reliable nanny in another and a third for general factotum."

"A waste of money," she said despondently as they went back to the car.

"Your brother's money," he pointed out consolingly. "Seeing him around, as I've done once or twice lately, I wouldn't have said he had any worries, domestic or otherwise."

"He had, for a time."

"And now he's handed them over to you?"

"In a way. He's one of those people — lucky or not, depends on how you look at it — who's wrapped up in his job and doesn't give his mind to much outside it."

"Does he hope his wife will come back?"

"No."

"Does he think she will?"

"He's quite certain she won't."

"I see. As you've never been up to Downing House, I'll take you the long way round; then you'll be able to see it in what used to be its surroundings. In front was the park — now owned by the golfers of the town. But there's still a lot of land on the other side."

They skirted the golf course. When they were near the woods on the far side of it, he stopped before a gateway decorated with iron tracery.

"This imposing entrance," he said, "was built in 1780, when one of my forebears had an attack of what's known as *folie de grandeur*. His name was Sinjon, spelled the wrong way — the only one in the family ever to bear the name until it was given to me, spelled the right way. The Downings had always been farmers, but this Sinjon made up his mind to put them on the social map. So he turned the land on this side into a park, and Downing Farm became Downing Park. This gate was planned as the main entrance. He even began to build a lodge or gatehouse — you can still see the foundations on the other side of the gate. But he died before it could get off the ground."

He drove on until he reached a narrow turning. Passing under an ivy-mantled archway, he spoke again.

"This was the original entrance to the original house. It was built close to the three cottages from which the first Downings issued. If I turned right at the fork ahead, we'd come to the house — but I'll take you to the cottages first. Two of them are empty; the third is occupied by an old couple who've been running the last remnants of the farm."

The road widened and divided; he turned left and soon the woods ended and fields began. Natalie saw pasture on one side and root crops on the other. A few cows were grazing. There was a large duck pond, an open barn and, beyond it, three thatched cottages. At one of these, Henry drew up. An old man appeared at a window and then opened the door and uttered a quavering welcome.

"Good to see you, Mr. Henry, sir. It's been a long time."

"Over a year," Henry agreed. "Natalie, this is my oldest friend, Jim Crouch. Where's your wife, Jim?"

"I'm here, I'm here." Mrs. Crouch's voice was shrill but firm. "Where else would I be but here? It's good to see you, Mr. Henry. I was feeding the hens round the back. Come inside, come inside, do."

They followed her into a small firelit kitchen.

"I brought Miss Travers to see you," Henry told the old couple. "Natalie, Mrs. Crouch brought me up."

"You may well say so," Mrs. Crouch remarked. "As soon as he was old enough to get here on his own, miss, he never left us till he was fetched. I used to have him round my feet, day in, day out. Sit down, miss. Will you take a cup of tea?"

Natalie thanked her but refused any refreshment.

"It's good to have visitors," the old man said. "We don't see many people nowadays. I was born near here, miss, but I worked for the Downings all my life. There'll be nobody to take over when I'm dead."

"That's true," said Mrs. Crouch. "It used to be a pretty place, Mr. Henry, in your granddad's time. Pigs and poultry, gallons of milk, vegetables, potatoes. And honey. We couldn't keep that up, not all alone."

"I could have done more if I'd had more help," said Mr. Crouch. "But you can't get farm lads anymore, and if you could, they wouldn't come to this place to live in these cottages. You've got to give 'em a regular villa nowadays, as well as pay 'em in gold and three days' holiday a week. And now the three ladies have gone from the big house. They came down here, Mr. Henry, and said good-bye."

"Now they say the golfers are going to get the house, which they shouldn't," said Mrs. Crouch, "because there's a new Downing over at the school, and he ought to have a chance to keep it."

"What'll he want with it?" her husband asked her. "He's a little I-talian. He'll want to go back and live in the sunshine."

As they drove away, Natalie asked who had lived in the other two cottages.

"People who worked up at the house," he answered.

"Did they walk there and back every day?"

"Yes. It's an easy walk — there's a short cut through the woods."

The road had widened; they were driving along a beech avenue. They passed a small lake, and then the drive curved. There were two more curves, and then the house was before them. Henry stopped and switched off the engine.

"Well?" he asked. "What do you think of it?"

For some moments she was too surprised to answer. She did not know quite what she had expected, but it was certainly not this beautiful stone-built building. She had heard only of its inconveniences and the probability that it was to be sold.

"It's . . . it's lovely," she said inadequately.

He began to speak in an imitation of a guide's monologue.

"Built in local stone by a farmer named Jasper Downing, in the year 1631. The plan is rectangular. The principal entrance is a flight of steps leading to a central doorway opening into a vaulted vestibule. Wood panelling from floor to ceiling in many of the rooms. The staircase has an elaborate scrollwork balustrade." He resumed his normal tones. "Perhaps it would have been smaller if Jasper had had a smaller family. But he had fourteen children. He also had several hundred acres of land to which he added and to which his son and all subsequent generations of sons added, until they possessed a goodly portion of the countryside."

"Why did he build here? Why not somewhere back among those lovely woods or overlooking the lake?"

"He built facing his broad acres, his lush pastures. There was no park. The park didn't come until Sinjon put it there. After that little uprush of showing off, his descendants seemed disposed to forget him and revert to their former humble state. Downing Park became Downing House. But the park was there, with its deer, to remind them that they were now gentlemen — so they compromised and became gentlemen farmers. In time they began to sell land. The town was born and became large and thriving. The Downings grew rich. And richer. But all they did was stash away their dough and go on farming. I'm sorry to say that they made no contribution whatever to the town's hall of fame. The new-mown hay, the clover, the smell of the warm, steaming cow sheds at dawn — those were their sole interests. They didn't join rebel causes; they didn't man the nation's fighting ships; they didn't waste time reading books or looking at pictures. The sons might go away, but they all came back, sooner or later, even if it was only in a coffin, like my father."

He got out of the car and opened her door.

"Come and see the inside."

They entered a large, beautiful vaulted hall, so cold that Natalie shivered.

"Rather a big place to warm," he commented. "Fireplaces in every room, but towards the end, nobody to light them. There was electric light, but no gas. Water, but not piped water. No coal, but wood unlimited if you cared to gather it and chop it. This" — he opened a door — "was the room in which my grandfather spent his days. And in the end, nights. It connected with this smaller room in which Aunt Blanche slept, so as to be at hand if he wanted anything. This is the sitting room that Clarice and Geraldine used. They weren't at home much. When they'd fin-ished doing war work, they took charge of the children's section of the public library. They've only recently given that up. Now they're living in the annex of the hotel. The kitchen — this way — is the same as it was when cooks rolled up their sleeves and produced large meals for large families and a multitude of farmhands."

"All this remaining furniture — you're selling it?"

He hesitated.

"When your niece Rowena tripped me up, I was trying to work out a problem: to sell or not to sell? Come in here, and I'll show you something."

She followed him to a room opening off the kitchen. In a corner stood four large trunks.

"See those? They were up in one of the attics. I looked inside without much interest — I'd had to get rid of so much accumulated junk when the aunts moved out. But then I saw that the four trunks were filled with papers. Letters, cuttings from old newspapers, photographs. And bills. Records, deeds, figures. They weren't miserly, those early Downings, but they obviously liked to keep a check on outgoings. Every detail — payments to masons, to carpenters, plasterers, all written down, all totalled up, a complete record of what this place cost to build and to keep in good repair. With some additional notes of a personal kind: a workman or a foreman ill, a workman's wife in labour, two children found hiding in a half-finished cellar. It's incredible to think how much they spent, and for so long, in keeping the house in good condition — without spending anything on bringing it up to date. What you see now is what Jasper and his family saw when they lived here."

She was standing looking down at one of the trunks he had opened.

"These look like letters," she said.

"They are."

"Didn't your aunts ever go through them, sort them, put them into bundles?"

"No. I found them and spent nearly a day looking through them. And I wished I hadn't, because it brought me up against the problem I mentioned to you: to sell or not to sell?"

"The furniture?"

"No. The house."

He said no more. He closed the trunk, and they went back to the car and drove away. She was silent for a time and then put a question.

"Do you mean that you're thinking of keeping the house?"

He did not answer for a time. When he did, it was in an abstracted manner.

"Have you ever been in the position in which you know you've taken a decision, but you still can't make up your mind to put it into words?"

"I think so. But —"

"Your brother's a golfer. He must have told you that they've been after this house ever since the town bought the park and turned it into a golf course."

"Yes, he told me."

"When I came to England with Leo, all I intended to do was put him into school, stay for a week or so and then leave. But on the way here I put in a week with Leo in London, showing him round. While we were there, I got the news that Blanche had married. I knew that would mean the end of Clarice and Geraldine's occupation of the house; they wouldn't or perhaps they couldn't stay on alone. They all got out, and they took their furniture. The house was empty. I was free to sell it."

"But —"

"But I'd begun asking myself why I was bringing Leo to school here. I knew my father wanted him to come, but he'd left it to me to make the final decision. Every Downing had been educated in Downinghurst; this was simply carrying on the tradition. Leo's mother was dead against it, but I decided to bring him because I was beginning to understand that only here, in this town, did our family mean anything. Three hundred years, plus. To sell, to walk out, to leave the house, was to give up our only claim to continuity. And so . . . to sell or not to sell?"

"And you've decided not to sell?"

"Yes."

"So what are you going to do with it?"

"I thought I ought to begin by spending some money on getting it habitable by today's standards. Then I can use it if I want to. And if Leo ever showed any signs of being a Downing, we could both spend some time in it. Perhaps all

I'm doing is procrastinating — I don't know. All I'm certain about is that I feel better now than I did in London, when I was struggling to make up my mind. This is the first time I've brought the thing into the open and clarified it. Thank you for listening."

"When are you going to let people know it isn't for sale?"

"I asked the golf committee to give me a month in which to think it over. They agreed." He gave her a half-apologetic glance. "And that's enough about me. Now you."

"Me? My roots are on a Brighton pavement."

"You were born there?"

"And went to school there, and had a teaching job there. Which I gave up for a time, but may go back to. This isn't the way back to the garage."

"Yes, it is. This is the old route, which nobody uses now because they prefer tarmac to cobbles. I'm taking you through the oldest part of the town."

They were soon threading their way along narrow, twisted streets along which ancient buildings alternated with tall, modern ones.

"This is where the town began," he said. "Some of these streets, some of these little houses are worth preserving, but the town councillors are more interested in the new than the old. The only man who puts up a fight for the past is the headmaster. The rest of them have their mind fixed on sport: twelve new tennis courts finished last spring, a new swimming pool you could use for the Olympics, four new sports fields ready for the soccer and rugger and cricket enthusiasts. All fine in its way, but it takes people's minds off what's happening to their town."

"Do you mind much what happens to it?"

"Yes, I do. What makes you think I don't?"

"The fact that you visit it so seldom. Where do you live?"

"I've got a kind of base in my stepmother's house in Florence, but most of the time I travel round Europe. My father got tired of having nothing to do when he went to live in Italy, so he started managing people's properties — buying, selling, renting. I inherited the business. I used to think it was the ideal job; now I'm not so sure."

They had reached the garage at which she had left her car, but neither of them made a move to get out.

"What do you do when you're in Brighton?" he asked.

"Work, do you mean? Or play?"

"Play."

"Swim and water ski and wind-surf in summer, ice skate at the rink in winter."

"You've got, gossip says, an apartment block all your own."

She laughed.

"All I've got is a house. It was large and rambling, and I decided to convert it. I asked an architect to come and look at it, but he wasn't much use because he didn't know the place as I did — for instance, I knew that a bathroom could be made out of two deep cupboards that were back to back in two of the upstairs bedrooms, and I knew that . . . well, it's not interesting. But I planned it myself in the end and got five sets of rooms out of it, besides the ones I keep for myself. Two of them are only one-room apartments, but they're nice, with miniature kitchens and bathrooms. It was fun seeing it all being done."

"And you could leave it to come here?"

"For a time. Do you think anybody'll answer those advertisements?"

"If they don't, I could help out as cook, snack variety. As I'm not selling the house, it looks as though I'll be around for some time, getting it modernized."

"Will your aunts be pleased to know you're not selling it?"

"Blanche will. I don't think the other two will care much. They're glad to be living in town — they always wanted to be in the center of things. Blanche is different — she likes a quiet life. I've had a summons to go and see Clarice and Geraldine. Would you come with me?"

"I'd like to meet them."

"Then let's go now."

He drove to the hotel, passed it and turned down a side street, on one side of which stood the three small chalets owned by the hotel and rented to permanent residents. Each stood behind a little paved courtyard. The one nearest to the hotel was joined to it by a short, curving colonnade. To this one Henry led Natalie. He addressed her as they were walking towards it.

"Don't write these two off as crazy," he said. "Wait a week or two before you decide."

He then knocked on a cream-painted door. It was opened by a large, handsome woman; behind her stood a smaller, slighter woman. Both, at sight of Henry, broke into loud exclamations of delight.

Natalie's first impression was that Nature had divided her gifts very unevenly between the two. Geraldine had a full, powerful-looking body, a noble nose, a billowing bosom and luxurious hair worn in upswept, Edwardian style. Clarice, a year younger and three inches shorter, had a meager frame, stringy hair, a negligible nose and no bosom whatsoever. Her voice was reedy; Geraldine's boomed. It was booming now.

"Henry, my dear boy! Such a pleasure!"

"Hello, Aunt Geraldine. I've brought a friend. Miss Travers."

"Come in, come in. I'm so glad to see you, Miss Trammers. Do come in. Sit down, both of you. Have you had tea?"

"No, but —"

"Then you must have some. Clarice, don't just stand there, dear. Telephone to the hotel for two cups. We had ours at half past four, Henry, but it'll be no trouble to make some more."

"Look, Aunt Geraldine, there's really no need —"

"Clarice dear, there was no need to explain *why* you wanted the cups. All you had to do was give the order. Where did you put the tea?"

"Tea?"

"The little green packet."

"We finished that."

"We have other packets. I bought four, and we've only used one. One from four leaves three; therefore, there are three packets left. Find them, dear."

"Did you look in the china cupboard?"

"Why in the world would packets of tea be in a . . . Yes, here they are. You don't take sugar, I know, Henry. Miss Trammers? If you wanted sugar, I could telephone for some, and they wouldn't be a moment sending it over. That is, they *shouldn't* be a moment, but do you know, I've found that the simplest request takes an age to be attended to. Like these two cups — you heard your aunt Clarice telephone for them? And where are they? What is easier than for an employee to put down a telephone, walk to the kitchen, pick up two cups and saucers and bring them the few yards to this annex? Well, we shall exercise patience. Or better still . . . Clarice dear, do run over and get them. Take this little tray to put them on. And don't stop to chat, as you usually do. So apt to get into conversation with people," she confided to Henry and Natalie as her sister went out. "Then she doesn't know how to break away. Sit on this chair, Henry, it's more comfortable. I'm so sorry" — she addressed

Natalie — "I've forgotten what Henry said your name was."

Natalie was about to tell her when from the colonnade came the sound of breaking china. Geraldine opened the door, looked out and gave an exclamation of annoyance.

"Clarice, really! Can't you carry two cups and saucers without dashing them to the ground?"

Henry was outside, picking up the pieces. Clarice stood by, muttering apologies. A hotel employee brought two more cups and took away the fragments.

"It was really not my fault," Clarice explained earnestly on returning to the sitting room. "I was going in, the man was coming out, I lifted the tray to take the things from him and they slid off."

"They'll slide onto the bill with all the other breakages," Geraldine said resignedly. "Now we'll make the tea."

"Let me," offered Henry.

"No, no, no; sit still, dear boy. I'll do it. Clarice, where is the kettle?"

"Kettle?"

"Yes, dear. An object which heats water. Kettle."

"Oh. It's in the bathroom. Don't you remember? You were going to boil some more water for our tea, but then you changed your mind."

"So I did. Well, fetch it, dear. Matches. Matches . . . Henry, have you matches?"

120

"I've got a lighter." He lit the gas below a tiny gas ring. The kettle was brought, empty, and Clarice was sent back to the bathroom to fill it.

"Water on, tea at hand, we now wait for the water to boil."

"There are only two cups," Clarice pointed out.

"Of course. Two people, two cups, Clarice dear."

"There are four people." Clarice pointed them out. "You, me, Henry and Henry's friend."

"You and I had our tea. At half past four, don't you remember?"

"Wasn't that yesterday?"

"How could it have been yesterday? Yesterday we went to tea with Mrs. Rowse."

"I thought that was tomorrow."

"Well, it's no use getting into an argument. We shall know when tomorrow comes. Now sit down and talk to Henry and his pretty friend. Henry, could you perform a second introduction? The name has slipped my mind."

"Natalie Travers," said Natalie.

"Travers . . . Travers . . . I think you must have some relations here, haven't you? Clarice, we know some Travers, don't we? That nice woman with the clever son at Oxford."

"That's Mrs. Rivers."

"So it is. Then do I mean the general and his wife, over at Spode?"

"They're the Jaggers."

"Natalie's brother is music director at

Downninghurst," said Henry.

"I knew there was *some*one. When one travels," Geraldine told Natalie, "one frequently comes upon connections one's known nothing about. Like the time my sister and I were staying for a time up in North Berwick, and we found no fewer than three Downings within a mile of us. They were no connection, but the *coincidence* was there. Now this music Travers at the school; if you were staying long enough to make inquiries, you might —"

"My brother."

"Oh, dear me, dear me!" Both Geraldine and Clarice thought this extremely amusing. "No, no, no; you mustn't expect the arm of coincidence to stretch quite as far as *that.* But you might find he was some distant cousin or something of that kind. If you wanted to find out, Henry could put you in touch; he knows everybody at the school. The kettle's boiling. No, Clarice, let me. I knew Henry likes his tea rather strong; he'll have to wait a little while for it to brew. And you? May I call you Natalie? Do you like it weak, strong or just as it comes? Such a pretty name, Natalie. I don't know any other Natalies."

"Yes, you do. That's Lady Pearce's name," said Clarice.

"No, it isn't, Clarice. She's called Amy. Amy Pearce. No, not Pearce. He died and she remarried and now she's Mrs. Something or other, Mrs. . . . Oh, Clarice, you are clever!"

"I knew I was right. I'm usually right."

"But not always, dear. I did have to point out to you only this morning that a recession is not something you sing in church. But you were right about Amy Pearce. She's now Mrs. Hatterley. Not Natalie, Hatterley. Now we've got that cleared up."

Henry thought that this might be the moment for him to find out why he had been sent for.

"You asked me to look in and see you, Aunt Geraldine."

"I did?"

"Yes."

"Then there must be something I want to talk to you about. Clarice, do you know what it could have been?"

"Yes. The desk."

"The . . . Oh, yes." Geraldine's brow darkened. "The desk." She put down the cup of tea she had been about to hand to Henry and spoke in tones of reproach. "*That,* Henry, is something I shall require you to explain. Did you or did you not know that your aunt Blanche had taken away from the house your grandfather's writing desk?"

"Yes, I knew. Could I have my tea?"

"Never mind about tea. You knew? You allowed her to take it?"

"You'd told me that you and Aunt Clarice didn't want anything else out of the house."

"We took what was ours. Do you realize that everything that your aunt Blanche took will in

123

time find its way into the possession of that man?"

"Her husband?"

"Whoever or whatever he is. She's keeping him well out of sight, you know. Nobody has so much as set eyes on him."

"I have," Henry said. "Twice."

There was a pause during which both his aunts struggled not to ask the question. Then they asked it in unison.

"What is he like?"

"Not very tall. Grey-haired. Not handsome, but what Grandfather would have called of good appearance. Scholarly. Why don't you three stop quarrelling and get together?"

"My dear Henry" — Geraldine spoke with a finality there was no mistaking — "you mustn't even *suggest* it. Blanche walked out and never came back. She said no word, gave us no warning of her intention to marry. She turned her back on us. I shall never forgive her."

"Nor shall I," said Clarice. "As far as I'm concerned, she's dished herself."

"I hope I'm not a person who bears grudges," Geraldine went on, "but she really let us down badly. We had spoken of buying a nice little house we could all share. When she bought that house overlooking the golf course, we naturally supposed that it would be for us all. But no. So it's no use speaking to me of olive branches. But if she's going to help herself to items of furniture that don't belong to her, you must stop her, Henry."

124

"She doesn't want anything more."

"I'm glad to hear it. And now I'm going to ask you, when you get an opportunity, to speak to the hotel manager about certain things we're finding very unsatisfactory. The service is really not what we expected, considering the price we pay for this cottage. Interminable delays every time we want to make an outside telephone call."

"Cats yowling on the roof every night," said Clarice. "And if we don't want to go over for dinner and ask them to send it here, stone cold."

"You may think these minor problems, Henry, but they make all the difference to our comfort. And now let me give you another cup of . . . but you haven't drunk your first cup."

"You didn't give it to me."

"You should have reminded me. One can't remember everything, my dear boy."

Henry was on his feet, signalling an appeal to Natalie.

"We have to go, I'm afraid," he said.

"Wait just for a moment. Clarice, where are those tickets?"

"I put them in the desk."

"Well, they're not there now. You must have . . . yes, here they are. Tickets, Henry, for the piano recital we've arranged in the hotel next week."

The tickets were written in red ink and announced that one person would be admitted to the Chopin recital to be given by Monsieur Louis du Boulay. He happened, Geraldine explained, to be paying a brief visit to Downing; hearing of this, she had written to him and asked if he would play for the town's charitable funds.

"You don't pay me now; you pay as you go in," she told Henry. "The B minor Scherzo — you mustn't on any account miss it. Take a ticket for Natalie, too. Natalie, are you staying here long?"

"No."

"That's a great pity. Come and see us while you're here. I've told Henry that any friends of his will always be welcome. Good-bye, good-bye."

"Well?" Henry asked when they were outside.

"Well what?"

"What do you think of them? Eccentric or just plain nut cases?"

"Just two old ladies living in the manner to which they've been accustomed."

"You sound as though you like them."

"I do. All that's wrong with them is that they're not in the least self-conscious. They just —"

"— act naturally. They certainly do."

Natalie's car was waiting at the garage. They walked inside to pay the bill.

"Thank you for filling in those two hours," she said.

"Can I drop in and see you at any time?"

"If you want to."

She said good-bye and drove to Julian's house,

where she found Miss Drew ready to leave.

"All in order," she reported. "Did you see those cinema posters?"

"No. I didn't go that way."

"I haven't time to stop and look at the things you've bought for the twins. I'll go through them next time I come. I had a bit of spare time, so I gave Mr. Travers's room a going over."

"Oh, but he hates his things touched!"

"If he lets them lie around any longer, nobody'll want to touch them. I told the squire straight out, I said, when we're married, he's got to keep his things decent. See you next week, same day, same time, right?"

"Well . . ."

"Oh, Mrs. Gilling phoned. Twice. First time to say she thought she'd found someone, second time to say she hadn't. But don't worry; she'll get you someone in the end. She got me my job at the school — she comes from Devon, did you know? She heard of me through a relation of hers in Torquay and she got me up here for an interview and I got the job. By the way, I made myself a hot supper, hope you don't mind, and I thought I ought to have an extra bite of something to keep me going in the cinema, so I cut some bread and slapped some ham on it, things like that, but I've left everything tidy. About your brother's room: He had food up there. You shouldn't let him start that. First it's tins, then it's plates of stuff and soon you'll have the room in a real mess. So long."

When she had gone, Natalie went round the house. The dining room had been put into impeccable order. The twins were in their night-clothes in their cot, ready to be tucked in. Julian's room looked unfamiliar; the furniture had been moved round. She did not think he would be grateful. In the kitchen all was tidy, and there were no surprises: the ham had been finished; there was bread enough and milk enough for the twins, but no more. The empty tin of French liver pâté was in the garbage pail.

For a few moments she wondered whether Julian's suspicions were justified; it was a lot of food to get through in an afternoon; she might have taken some away. But remembering Miss Drew's athletic strides, bulging muscles and open-air exercise on her bicycle, she put the thought aside. Mrs. Drew had been right; her daughter needed filling.

Julian telephoned later to say that he would not be home to dinner.

"Sorry I can't make it. Have you got enough stuff in the house to make yourself a meal?"

"Yes."

"I'll probably be late. Don't wait up."

She put down the receiver. He had not asked after the twins. He would undoubtedly ask, to-morrow, about his liver pâté. She would tell him that she had eaten it.

The telephone rang as she was coming down-stairs after settling the twins in bed. Answering, she heard Mrs. Wray's voice.

"I'm so sorry to disturb you — were you with the children?"

"No."

"I wanted to ask you if you'd very kindly take in the milk bottles from my door for the next week. I'm just off to join my husband — we're going to have a week in London. Would it be too much bother?"

"Of course not. Can I do anything else while you're away?"

"No, thank you. Henry has the keys. He wouldn't stay in the house while I was away, but he promised to keep an eye on it. Have you had any luck about domestic help?"

"Not yet."

"Henry told me you'd advertised. I do hope something comes of it. Good-bye. I hope to see you in a week."

And that, Natalie mused, putting down the receiver, changed her own plans for the evening; she had intended to go next door for a brief visit after dinner. At home in Brighton, she would have been able to put through a call to any one of a wide circle of friends, and the problem of how to spend the evening would have been solved. Here . . . well, there were the twins, and there was television; what more did any woman need to help her pass a lonely evening?

But it was not, after all, to be a lonely evening. Half an hour later there was a summons from the front door. She answered it to find Henry Downing on the doorstep.

Chapter

6

His arms were full of packages. He stepped in without waiting for an invitation, walked to the kitchen and lowered them onto the table.

"Supper," he announced. "Supper for two — you and me. The shops were shut, but the pubs were open. Ham sandwiches, beef sandwiches, sausage rolls. And" — he produced it from his pocket — "a bottle of red wine." He leaned forward and kissed her lightly. "And thou," he added. "Thou and I. Beneath the hough."

Was that kiss, she wondered, merely a friendly salute, a fleeting greeting? Or was it something on account — a promise of better things to come? There was nothing in his manner that could provide an answer. He was putting a question of his own.

"How are our twins?"

"Our twins are asleep."

"Good. What am I doing here, you were about to ask? Incidentally, you shouldn't open the front door after dark without putting your lips to the crack and saying, 'Who and what are you?' Suppose I'd pushed past you with a stocking over my face?"

"You were about to tell me what you were doing here."

"Aren't you pleased to see me?"

"It depends what you're doing here."

He was opening parcels and putting the contents onto plates which he took from a cupboard.

"It's a long story," he said. "I was sitting in the hotel lounge, thinking about you and marvelling at the fate which had thrown us together on this urban island. I moved to the bar, ordered a drink and sat watching the diners drifting into the restaurant. By twos and by threes they went, and by fours. You do like mustard on your sandwiches? Good. Suddenly my attention became fixed on one of the tables near the door. Four men, all eating heartily. Two of them unknown to me. The third, Leo's housemaster. The fourth . . . your brother, Mr. Julian Travers. I don't think that's a name to give a harmless music director; it belongs to melodrama. Where do we eat?"

"In the drawing room. You were saying?"

"Yes, your brother. Dining. Feasting. And where were you? At home looking after the twins. You were alone. I was alone. You'd told me that your brother was in the habit of taking home food. If he hadn't gone home, he hadn't taken any food. So I brought what you see here, so that you and I could eat together. Are you grateful? Are you hungry? Do you want my company, or shall I gather up the feast and go and look for some other woman to share it with me?"

"I'd rather you didn't take the food with you. That wine will be too cool to drink."

"We'll *chambré* it."

131

The telephone rang. She picked up the receiver, listened for a moment and then placed it noiselessly on the table. He stared at it in astonishment, and she motioned him towards the drawing room.

"If you don't want to talk," he asked, "why don't you ring off?"

"It's Mrs. Gilling. She phones through reports several times a day. She doesn't notice that there's nobody at the other end."

"I see." He was looking round the room. "Pity you haven't a fireplace. Do you have fireplaces in your house in Brighton?"

"No. Nice modern heating."

"You'll be sorry one day, when the world has run out of oil or we can't afford to buy it. We'll have to go back to wood chopping, and people will flock to visit me because when it's cold, I settle myself in front of a roaring fire and make toast, and butter it while it's hot so that the butter drips down my chin when I'm eating it."

She went back to the kitchen, said, "Thank you so much for phoning," replaced the receiver on its stand and returned to the drawing room. Henry had placed the bottle of wine close to one of the radiators and was turning it slowly to take the chill off. He had also, she noted gratefully, taken off the slight chill that had settled on her at the prospect of a long and lonely evening. She felt warm, happy and relaxed — too relaxed to take the trouble to analyze his manner, which was a mixture of casualness and intimacy.

132

Seated opposite her, the food and the bottle of wine between them, he opened the conversation by referring to his aunts.

"I'm glad you liked Clarice and Geraldine."

"They surprised me," she said. "I knew they were in their seventies. I didn't expect them to be so . . . so full of energy."

"Most of it misapplied. Like the recital they've arranged for Louis du Boulay. There'll be a message from him in a day or two to say he can't come to Downing after all."

"Then why did he agree to give a recital?"

"Well, it goes like this: Clarice glances at the lists of concerts in the *Times* and says: 'What a pity nobody ever comes to perform in Downing.' So Geraldine says: 'We must invite somebody.' So they do. While they're waiting for a reply, they book a room for the celebrity at the hotel and issue tickets for the recital. The reply comes: the celebrity regrets. So no recital, but a lot of pleasant anticipation and excitement for Clarice and Geraldine. Can you find anything wrong with that?"

"Well . . ."

"Quite right. Nobody could. Two harmless old ladies building harmless little fantasics. I'm enjoying this intimate little party — are you?"

"I'm enjoying the sandwiches."

The sandwiches finished, he would have liked to settle down with her on the sofa, with the rest of the wine at hand. But when they had cleared away the few plates they had used, Natalie made herself comfortable in a low chair.

"There's room here." He patted the sofa. "You look unfriendly over there."

"I'm fine. Go on talking."

"Questions first. Will you agree that we've been, as I said earlier, thrown together?"

"We're both here on missions, I suppose — but we don't expect to be here very long. As far as I can gather when I see Leo, he has no complaints, so you can leave him. You've also solved your problem of not selling your house, so you're free to go back to Italy. When those advertisements produce some applicants, I'll be free, too. The difference between us is that I have to occupy the waiting period in working, whereas all you've got to do is waste time."

"Waste time? Is that what I've been doing this evening after all that outlay on food and wine? Is it wasting time to try to further our brief but unusually promising acquaintance? Was the earlier part of today — the afternoon and early evening — of less significance than I took it to be? Marooned as you and I are, for however short a time, are we to occupy separate ends of our atoll and ignore the need we both feel for company, each other's company? I'm not the one who's wasting time. You are."

"You've made your decision to keep the house. Don't you have to go back to work?"

"You weren't listening. On an atoll, I said. Marooned. Just the two of us. Why drag in work?"

134

"To remind you. Somebody must be waiting for you to go back and sign some letters."

"Nobody's waiting for me. Not even any women."

"None?"

"Nothing you could call serious. Living the way I do, I don't meet nice, steady, home-loving girls. If they're clients, they're rich and on the loose, looking for a villa for a season or two. If they're women I meet after office hours, they're living it up with rich protectors. Tell me something: Could you live in this town?"

"Downing?"

"Yes. Could you settle down here, live your life here, be a permanent denizen of Downing?"

"You certainly couldn't. You've always been anxious to make a quick getaway."

"That was when there was nothing to stay for. Please will you come and sit here?"

He leaned forward and put out a hand. She took it, and he drew her out of her chair to a place beside him on the sofa.

"That's better," he said. "Now I can hear you more clearly. What I want to say is —"

He stopped. A knock had sounded on the front door — timid, but after a few moments repeated more loudly.

"Not your brother; he'd have a key. Visitors?"

She had glanced out of a window. A woman was standing on the top step — a woman in a shabby coat, nervously clutching a handbag.

"I'd say an applicant for one of the jobs. But

the paper won't be out until tomorrow."

"Don't let anyone escape. I'll wait in here, and you can come back and report."

Natalie opened the front door. The woman's skin was dark; her age, perhaps fifty. She gave an uncertain smile.

"Miss Travers?"

"Yes."

"I have come" — the voice was soft, but somewhat nasal and singsong — "because I heard that you are wanting someone to work."

"Will you come in?" Natalie led the way to the dining room. "Please sit down."

"Thank you. I am Mrs. Swayne. It is spelled in this way: S-w-a-y-n-e. I am from India, but long ago. I heard that you are looking for someone to look after some children, and I said to myself that I would come and see you because I am not happy in the work I am doing now. All day long I am sitting in a cage, shut up, and long hours and not much pay because it is my brother-in-law's shop and it has only started a few months ago and you have to wait for people to know about it, isn't it?"

"You work in a shop?"

"A very nice shop, Miss Travers. I hope you will go there to buy things. It is Hamil's — it is near the baker's shop in Regent Lane, you know?"

"No. I'm afraid I don't know much about the town."

"The shop sells many things, this and that, it is

as you might call it a grocer's, but also it has Indian spices. I don't serve there in it. I am the cashier. I sit near to the door, and I take the money when people are going out. At first I was in the open, but some robbers came one day, right in the middle of the afternoon, and took away the money, so after that my brother-in-law, Mr. Hamil, said it is better to put wire round. For protection."

"I see."

"But one day in the shop I heard a lady talking about you. She said you had come to look after your brother's house and his children, but you had to go away, so you wanted someone in your place. So I thought: I am a mother, I brought up my two sons and I loved them and looked after them well, and that is what I would like to do if you gave me this job. My sons are grown up now. They didn't like it here, so they went to India."

There was a pause.

"I don't know whether you know the age of my brother's children," Natalie said. "They're twins. They're only thirteen months old."

"So small?"

"I'm afraid so."

"I thought that they were older, but what is this difference? None. My sons were babies once. And that is not all I can do, Miss Travers. I am a good cook, especially Indian cookery; say anything you like in that way, and I can make it. I would have liked to cook for Mr. Hamil, but his mother came and said no, she would live with

137

him and do it. Also, I can look after old people, if you have old people. I was only ten years when my mother and father brought me and my sister from India, and we lived with some cousins in London and I went to school with my sister, and then we both helped to teach English to more children coming from India and not knowing anything. I got married, but after I had two sons, my husband died. My sister got married to Mr. Hamil. Then my father and mother got ill, and they were old also, and I looked after them, cooking and cleaning and everything. Mr. Hamil and my sister were in London first, and then they came to open this shop, but my sister died, and my father and mother had died and I was alone, so Mr. Hamil said to come and live here and have a home with him and work in the shop. I am forty-four years, I don't know whether you think this is too old, but I am strong and I keep good health, you know? And I will be honest with you, Miss Travers, it was all right before Mr. Hamil's mother came to live, but now there is no room for me upstairs, and I don't like sleeping behind the shop with no water to wash and no place to keep my dresses and that. If you would take me on, I would work hard for you."

Natalie studied her. Black hair parted at the side and worn in a coiled plait at the back of her head. Large dark brown eyes. A manner that in spite of nervousness held dignity. Her hands were clutching the handbag more tightly.

"I wouldn't want much money, Miss Travers.

That is the least of it. It is not to earn more money that I would like to come, only to be in a house, a home, with children." A tear began to course slowly down one cheek. She ignored it. "I know that your brother will be alone when you go away. I would look after him well. I have done washing, ironing, I used to press my sons' suits, I am good at that. If you wanted me and I had to say to my brother-in-law that I am leaving his shop, he will be angry because he wrote to me in London and said come and I will give you a home. But since his mother is there, there is no place for me, so where is this home? All day I am in the shop, and when it closes, I count the money and then I arrange the goods for next day and then I go upstairs and I am fed. Have you given your job to someone else?"

"No."

"Then?"

Natalie sat trying to think of something to say. Probably competent, certainly kind, certainly trustworthy. But . . . she wouldn't do. Her voice would get on Julian's nerves. She had doubtless cooked savoury messes for her sons, but she would consider Miss Drew's chart inadequate and too rigid. She would be invaluable for a family of three-to-sevens; motherly, indulgent. But in this house, with Julian more often out than in, with nobody to supervise, nobody to explain the routine . . . No.

She opened her mouth to say so and heard, instead, a far-from-discouraging tone.

139

"I would have to talk this over with my brother, Mrs. Swayne. He —"

"I would get references, isn't it? Even if Mr. Hamil was angry and wouldn't speak for me, I know some people in London, good people; you could ask them, and they would tell you it is all right. My father was in the railways in India until the British went away. I have got letters, old letters he brought with him when we came to England, telling that he is all right."

"I'd like to see them if we . . . if we came to an arrangement. But may we leave it for the present?"

"Please do not come to the shop to see me. Until anything is fixed, I wouldn't like Mr. Hamil to know about it, in case. If you want to see me, please tell the lady at the baker's shop at the corner."

Natalie rose. Mrs. Swayne walked slowly to the door, her back straight, only her hands showing her distress as they squeezed the cheap plastic of her handbag,

"Thank you for coming," Natalie said.

Mrs. Swayne went down the steps to the drive and then paused and looked back.

"Please, Miss Travers . . . No, nothing. Good night."

Natalie went slowly back to the drawing room. Henry spoke after a glance at her expression.

"No use?"

"No."

"Any particular reason?"

"She heard about the job through Mrs. Gilling. She's from India. She'd be kind to the twins, and she'd look after them well."

"But —"

"But Julian wouldn't like her. She wouldn't fit in. If this were a house big enough to give her a room, a kind of sitting-room near the twins . . . but there's only the spare bedroom I'm in, and she couldn't make a . . . a home in it. She's worked in a house, but only her parents' house. She's used to doing things her own way, and something tells me it isn't our way. And earrings, and rings, and brooches — nothing showy, but obviously part of her everyday attire. I couldn't picture her working here — but I liked her. I liked her very much, and I trusted her, somehow, and I can't bear to think of her going back to that hole behind the shop and being caged up all day and probably being snubbed by that ghastly mother of his and getting upstairs too late to join them at their meal and being handed a plate of leftovers. She was crying. Not crying, just one tear, and she took no notice and it just trickled down and fell onto the blouse she was wearing."

"Look, you mustn't —"

"It isn't as though she knew what she was coming to when she came to Downing. I suppose looking after her parents took most of whatever money there was, and when this brother-in-law wrote and asked her to come here, she thought it was kindness and didn't realize she was going to be . . . to be exploited. Now her two sons have gone back to India, and she's alone and stuck, with no home, and if she hasn't got a home she can't go out to work as a daily."

"Are you going to get as upset as this every time you interview an applicant?"

"I'm not upset," she said passionately. "I'm angry, that's all. Why should you and I be sitting here in comfort, with homes, wherever they are, with relations, whatever they're like, with everything we need, when that woman's just gone away to live without hope of any kind in her cage in that shop? People say there aren't enough good things to go round. That's a lie. There *are*. There are enough good things for everybody, if only people would share them out. But we've got too much, and she's got nothing, and I let her go without even asking if she'd like a lift. I just let her go. And she went knowing it was no good. I couldn't tell her, but she knew. I saw that she knew."

She paused. He watched her struggling back to self-control.

"You've got to prepare yourself for some more interviews like this one," he said gently. "Think of it this way: If you were a competent person who happened to be in need of a job, would you look for one in the Downing *Evening Weekly*?"

"No, I wouldn't."

"So what it amounts to is that you're scraping the bottom of the barrel. You may be lucky, but

142

if I were you, I wouldn't pin any hopes on finding hidden treasure. Or treasures. And you mustn't get worried when you have to turn down obviously unsuitable applicants." He came close to her, lifted his hand and gently stroked her cheek. "I'm sorry for this woman who came tonight, but if you're interested, she isn't the only one whose hopes were dashed. Mine were, too."

"What were you hoping for? Don't tell me."

"Only a crumb. One little crumb of encouragement." He led her back to the sofa. "I've known you all this time, but I don't feel that I've made the smallest impact. And I have a depressing feeling that you're not a girl who can be hurried. However, I'll persevere. Tomorrow's Saturday. Will you come on a picnic?"

"Picnic?"

"Indoor picnic. In my house. You can bring the twins. Will your brother mind if you're out all day on his free day?"

"He isn't free on Saturdays. It's the day he can get most done — he can get all the orchestras together. But I can't leave the house. Suppose people come in answer to those advertisements, notices?"

"They won't come before the evening. The weekly paper doesn't come out until six. So will you come?"

"Yes."

"Could you get up the house early? I'll be there at dawn, getting the house ready."

"Then you won't have time to get a picnic ready. I'll do it."

"Good girl. Leo's coming and bringing a friend. We'll need lunch and tea — I can leave those to you?"

"Yes."

"Do you think it's a good idea?"

"I'll tell you when I've tried it."

He went reluctantly to the door.

"I suppose it's time for me to go. I don't want to leave you to brood over the woman from India."

"I won't brood."

"Can I go up and look at the twins?"

"What do you want to do that for?"

"I've never seen twins asleep in their cot before. It seems to me to be a gap in my experience — or education."

"Go up if you want to."

"You come, too."

They went up together. He went into the twins' room and looked at the two sleeping forms and then came out and stood looking into the bedroom Natalie used.

"That window — it overlooks my aunt's house?"

"It doesn't overlook it, exactly. I can see her gate and a bit of the garden path."

"But not the whole house?"

"No. Only one window."

They went downstairs, and he paused in the hall.

"The pram," he said. "You'll need it for the twins tomorrow, but it won't fit into your car. I'll take it now."

He pushed it down the steps, opened the back door of his car and lifted it in. Then he came up the steps again.

"Forgot something," he said, and kissed her.

She watched his headlights out of sight and then closed the door — only to see more lights and hear the sound of a car on the drive. She opened the door again and saw Mrs. Gilling walking round to open the passenger's door and help a small, stout woman to alight. The two came up the steps together.

"I'm sorry to come at this hour," Mrs. Gilling said, "but as I told you on the phone, it was now or never. If I hadn't brought her to fix up things with you now, somebody else would have snatched her. This is Mrs. Lingford. I told you about her on the phone, but I thought you ought to talk to her."

Natalie took them inside.

"We can only sit down for a few minutes," Mrs. Gilling said. "This is Miss Travers, Mrs. Lingford. I know you two are going to get on. Nobody, Miss Travers, nobody could find a better worker than Mrs. Lingford. You're lucky to get her. As soon as I heard that old Mrs. Grant had died, I went hurrying round, and I was the first, wasn't I, Mrs. Lingford?"

Mrs. Lingford opened tightly pressed lips, said, "Second," and closed them again.

145

"I was the second," Mrs. Gilling went on. "I explained your situation to Mrs. Lingford, and I told her you'd put an advertisement in the weekly paper, but we agreed that we wouldn't wait to see if anybody answered. Even if you get any replies, which I doubt, they won't be any good. I know from experience. I'm still looking round to find someone who'll come and live in and take over the twins, but no luck so far, and you can't go on doing everything. Now you'll have Mrs. Lingford to do the housework. She's the best worker in Downing. She's not young" — Mrs. Lingford gave a wide, toothless grin — "but she's strong, and she's efficient. She charges more than other daily women, but that must be a secret between you and her. She can come every morning from nine to eleven."

"To half past," corrected Mrs. Lingford. "Not Saturday and Sunday neither. I come punctual at nine, and I get m'self a cupper at eleven. Nothing to eat. I like to work on a empty stummick. And I don't like to be told. I know what to do."

Natalie liked the look of her — she was diminutive, but doughty, and she sounded independent. Better still, she did not seem to be talkative. With her to take over the housework, there would be more time to spend with the twins.

"When could you start?" she asked.

"Monday as coming, nine sharp. I'll want a key in case nobody's up."

146

Natalie gave her a key. The terms were stated and agreed to. Mrs. Gilling, flushed with triumph, led her prize away. After seeing her into the car, she returned for a few words with Natalie.

"A treasure, a real treasure," she confided. "Eighteen years with old Mrs. Grant and not a day missed. I've been after her before, when Mrs. Grant's been away, but she wouldn't leave her. It was only by getting there so fast that I got my word in first — second — and told her about you, that she agreed to take you on. You're lucky, you really are."

"I'm very grateful. I hope she'll like the job. Good night, and thank you."

She was in bed when Julian came in. When he came upstairs, he knocked on her door.

"Not asleep?"

"No. Come in. Did you enjoy your evening?"

"Not much. I saw Downing in the bar. Someone said you'd been in his car earlier today. Were you?"

"Yes. He took me up to see his house."

"Did you find out what's going to happen to it?"

"He said the golf committee had given him a month to make up his mind."

"A lot of people think he isn't going to sell it."

She studied his gloomy expression and asked: "Is it so important?"

He was standing by the window.

"Important? Only to the golfers, and I don't

suppose they matter much. But it's a good course. It's so good that we're getting more and more first-class golfers coming to play here. But there's never been a clubhouse — only a small hut which was called temporary when it was put up ten years ago. If we could get Downing House, there'd be endless difficulties — mortgage, alterations — but if we found enough money, it would make all the difference to the club members. Somewhere comfortable to meet, to sit; a bar, a snack bar. Changing rooms. Showers. But if Downing's not going to sell, that's the end of that. Perhaps you could put our point of view to him — or aren't you seeing him again?"

"Yes. Tomorrow. You'll be out all day, won't you?"

"Yes. Well, I won't keep you from your sleep."

If he had asked where the pram was, she would have had to mention the picnic; as it was, she said nothing. A picnic at this time of the year, even an indoor picnic, might have elicited some unwelcome comment. She stopped him as he opened the door.

"Wait a minute, there's news. Mrs. Gilling brought round a daily woman, and I've engaged her."

"We tried dailies. None of them stayed."

"This one might. Her name's Mrs. Lingford and she —"

"Lingford? The Mrs. Lingford who works for old Mrs. Grant?"

"Worked. Mrs. Grant died."

"Mrs. Grant was alive at eleven o'clock this morning. I saw her out, doing her shopping."

"Well, she died. And Mrs. Gilling hurried round and got hold of Mrs. Lingford."

"Sounds ghoulish."

"Never mind about ghoulish. She's coming at nine on Monday."

"How long can she go on? She's on her last legs."

"She said she was strong, and I believe it. She's expensive, but I thought it was worth agreeing to the extra."

"What extra?"

"The extra she charges for being so efficient. I gave her a key."

"Well, don't be too hopeful. Good night."

He went out of the room, and she lay reflecting on the contrast in his tone when he spoke of the clubhouse and when he made a remark or two about Mrs. Lingford. Deep concern — and no concern.

She remembered her mother's surprise at his marriage; Julian, she had said, was a born bachelor. He appeared to have reverted to his bachelor ways and, as far as she could see, would soon forget that they had ever been interrupted.

Chapter

7

Natalie was up and out early on the following morning. She left the twins at breakfast with their father, who was instructed to put them into their playpen when breakfast was over. She drove to the shops and bought food for a picnic for four people. The day looked unpromising, so she included two cans of soup that she could serve if the sun failed to come out.

With the picnic basket packed and on the back seat of the car, and the twins beside her in front, she set off for Downing House. She hesitated at the iron gates and then decided to open them and approach the house by what Sinjon Downing had intended to make the main entrance. A short way inside the gate, she passed the half-concealed, overgrown foundations of what was to have been the lodge. The road ran between the golf course and the woods; after turning into a wide, rutted lane, she found herself facing the house. She drove round to the other side of it and came upon Leo and his friend, who was very small, very thin and very black. Henry came out of the house and helped lift the children out of the car.

"You know Leo," he said, "but you haven't met Joshua."

Joshua, who had been staring at the twins with eyes round with wonder, came forward and shook hands.

"I am from Nigeria," he told Natalie.

"Miss Travers," Henry told him, "is the sister of Mr. Travers, the school music director."

"I don't know him. He doesn't teach me any-thing," Joshua said. His eyes went to the picnic basket. "I can help you if you want to take out the things to eat."

"We won't be eating yet," Henry told him. "But let's get the stuff inside."

They went up the steps and entered the hall. Natalie stood looking round her with a surprise that rendered her speechless. Yesterday so bleak and bare, it now glowed with warmth. A huge fire crackled in the wide stone fireplace. Chairs and sofas were placed round it. A table stood close by. There were rugs on the floor and, in the center of the room, a large square carpet — for the twins to crawl on, Henry explained.

"Well, what do you think?" he asked.

"It's . . . it's wonderful. You must have got here early."

"Around dawn. I did the preliminaries and then went and fetched Leo and his chum and brought them back here to do some wood carrying."

"We got a wagon from a shed, and we put the wood into it and pushed it here," Leo said.

"Wheelbarrow," corrected Henry. "Don't settle down yet — we're going for a walk. The weather reports were pretty pessimistic for the afternoon's prospects, so we'll get some fresh air for the twins while we can. You and Joshua can put them into their pram."

For a moment Joshua, his eyes rolling in apprehension, seemed about to refuse. Then he summoned his resolution.

"I'll take the girl one," he told Leo. "You take the brother."

With the utmost care, he deposited Rowena in the pram and was rewarded by a piercing scream of rage.

"Whassa matter? What did I do?" he asked Natalie in panic.

"Nothing, Joshua." She raised her voice above the noise, to which Randall was now contributing. "It's just that you and Leo have put them on the wrong side. They'll have to be changed round."

The change effected, peace returned to the hall. The twins were warmly covered. Leo and Joshua looked for their anoraks and found them at the bottom of a pile of wood outside. The party was ready to set off.

"I can push them?" Joshua asked.

"You can if you keep within the speed limit," Henry answered.

Their walk was to the cottages which Natalie had seen the day before. The object of the exercise, Henry explained, was to introduce Leo to Mr. and Mrs. Crouch.

The old couple saw them approaching, came to meet them, took them into their cottage and gave each of the boys a large glass of milk. Mr. Crouch refused to agree that Leo looked Italian; he was, he declared, the image of his great-grandfather Rowland Downing, who was still alive when the Crouches first came to the cottage.

On the way to the house Leo remarked with some concern that the cottages needed repair. This surprised Joshua.

"In Nigeria," he said, "they would be for rich people. You should give one to my grandmother — her house is falling down. But it doesn't matter because it is not cold over there."

Leo was not interested in grandmothers.

"I'm hungry," he announced. "We had breakfast such a long time ago."

"Then let's get back and unload the picnic basket," Natalie suggested.

Back at the house, there was no need to allocate tasks. Henry went into one of the rooms and returned with a large tablecloth. The two boys carried the twins to the carpet, deposited them on it and hurried to the table on which Natalie was laying out food and drink. Henry, after a glance at the cans of soup, disappeared once more and this time returned with a small camping gas stove. Natalie left the three men to cut bread and make sandwiches while she took the twins one by one to the vast bathroom — it looked to her the size and shape of a tennis court — changed them and returned them to their rug. The fire roared; the table groaned; the twins

153

crawled to the table, grasped a leg and hauled themselves upright to get a better view of the preparations.

Leo and Joshua fed themselves and the twins. Natalie and Henry sat propped against sofa cushions, plates on their knees, drinks at hand.

"I've got news," she said out of a long silence. "I've got some help in the house. Mrs. Gilling brought a daily woman who's said to be a treasure."

"Permanent?"

"I hope so. She's very old and very small and rather fat. If she were a ship, you'd name her *Indomitable*. She's starting on Monday."

"Will she be able to look after the twins so that you can spend more time with me?"

"No."

"Pity. Was your brother relieved to know that part of the gap had been filled?"

"Of course." She spoke dryly. "He's been losing sleep, worrying. Now he'll be able to give all his time to golf and music." Her eyes went slowly round the hall, taking in the beautiful rugs and the soft colours of the carpet. "It was a good idea, this picnic."

"Keeping the house so as we could have one — that was a good idea, too."

"Julian asked me what was going to happen to the house. I told him what you told me — that the golf committee had given you a month. But he's heard rumours that you're not selling."

"I've heard no rumours, but I'm getting mean

looks from all the golfers I pass in the streets."
He raised his voice. "Leo, come here a minute."

Leo, a sandwich in each hand, came.

"Do you want to keep this house?" Henry asked him.

Leo waited until his mouth was empty.

"This house? This house we're in now?"

"Yes."

"Keep it? But it's ours already."

"We could sell it."

"Why? I was born here, wasn't I?"

"You were. So was I. I can remember the day you were born. It was summer, but it was a cold summer; your mother had planned her wardrobe by the calendar and not by the climate. She stayed in bed most of the time, to keep warm."

"Which was her room?"

"The one above this hall. That's where you were born. You didn't take long to arrive — your mother was only too anxious to get back to Italy."

"She didn't like it here. I know; she told me. And my father didn't like it either."

"I wasn't too keen on it myself for a time, but I've come to the conclusion that there's no place like home. Every time I think of somebody else occupying this house, I feel there's something wrong."

Leo looked at him for some moments in speculation.

"You're going to live here? In this house?" he asked.

"I'm thinking it over. But it's a bit of a barn."
Natalie spoke irritably.

"Why call it a barn? It's not a barn. It's a beautiful house, and if you want to live in it, all you have to do is use your imagination and make a few minor alterations. Why did anybody ever think of it as a clubhouse? It's not a clubhouse; it's a family house. You should take the fireplaces out of all those bedrooms, for a start. Then you can put in more bathrooms. You divide the kitchen and make half of it into a utility room: dishwashers, clothes washers and dryers, big double sinks and a marble slab to do the flowers on. And you put in the latest type of central heating. You build garages onto the back of the house, with a door leading into the room where those four trunks are — it can be made into a back hall for gardening boots and things."

There was a pause.

"No more minor alterations?" Henry asked.

"Those are the main ones. Then you'll have the lovely house your forefathers built in sixteen whatever-it-was, screened in front from the golfers and with a lovely stretch of private playground behind — or in front, whichever way you happen to be looking. And inside the house, warmth and comfort and up-to-date labour-saving equipment." She got to her feet and brushed the crumbs off her jeans. "How you could ever have thought of letting a place like this go, I can't understand. Clubhouse! Now I know how it was that your forebears went on living here and did nothing to bring it up to date. Inertia. And of course, they had servants to keep them warm and comfortable, and it didn't matter whether the servants were warm and comfortable or not. It's time to bed the twins down. Can I push those two big chairs together to make a cot?"

A cot was improvised. The twins were settled into it. Randall addressed a brief speech to his sister and fell asleep.

"We'll have to be quiet," Leo told Joshua.

"Then let's go outside."

"No. It's raining. We'll go upstairs."

They went upstairs, and silence fell on the great hall. Natalie had packed away everything but the tea, and was comfortably ensconsed against the cushions. Henry, having piled logs on the fire, lay back, watching her. The voices of the two boys floated down to them from time to time. The room was darkening, the fire throwing flickering light into its distant corners.

"What are you thinking about?" he asked after a time.

"I was thinking how easy it is to solve other people's problems."

"Could I solve yours?"

Her eyes were half closed; she answered lazily.

"I don't think so."

"It would be awkward if he followed you here."

Her eyes opened.

"Who?"

"Him. I'd challenge him to a duel, and one of us would be spitted. Blood all over the under-growth, and you wringing your hands. What's amusing you?"

"You. You talk more rubbish faster than anyone I ever met."

"A duel to the death is a very serious matter."

"You're sure there's a 'him'?"

"Could anyone look at you and doubt it? What's his name?"

That, she told herself, was going too far. That was an impertinent inquiry. Her business was her own. Her love life, if any, was her own. This was the moment to apply the freeze.

"Michael," she said.

"Michael." He repeated the name thought-fully. "In Hebrew, if I'm not mistaken, who is like God. Is he godlike?"

"No."

"Nine Byzantine emperors were named Mi-chael. Is he descended from one of them?"

"No."

"Then I don't know him. You'd better give him up and have me instead. Does the idea appeal to you?"

"I'll let you know when I've thought it over."

"Good. How long do you think you'll take to —"

He stopped, frowning. Leo and Joshua had come in, carrying between them a beautiful ivory box with an elaborately carved lid. They sat on the floor beside Henry and opened it.

"Look — chessmen," Leo said.

"Your grandfather's," Henry told him. "Carved to represent Chinese figures. Go and play chess with Joshua."

"He doesn't know how."

"If you come in here, you'll wake the twins."

"The other rooms are too cold to stay in. Miss Travers, do you play chess?"

"I daresay I play better than Henry does. Bring the box over here, and we'll teach Joshua."

Henry realized that the brief moments of intimacy were over. With a resigned air, he got up and went outside to fetch wood. The rain continued to pour down, increasing the sense of warmth and comfort indoors.

When it was time for tea, Henry produced two meter-long brass toasting forks, and the two boys made slice after slice of toast and passed them to Henry to be buttered. Not until the bread was finished did this pastime come to an end.

"Can't we do this again tomorrow?" Leo asked when it was time to go.

"You can; I can't," Natalie answered. "I have to stay at home with my brother. I don't see much of him during the week."

Henry settled her with the twins into her car.

"When I was out shopping for the picnic things this morning," she told him, "I drove past the shop — the shop Mrs. Swayne works in."

"Mrs. —"

"The woman who came."

"Oh, yes. The unsuccessful applicant for the job. Did you go into the shop?"

"No. But I saw her. And it's true — it's a cage she has to sit in, cheap chicken wire, with a hole to pass out change to the customers."

"You're going to get upset again. Go home and write a check and send it to a society for the benefit of other Mrs. Swaynes, and then you'll feel better."

"Checkbook generosity."

"The only kind possible to a number of people. And no checks, no charity organizations. Will you come here next Saturday?"

"Yes."

On the following day she found that as far as Julian was concerned, there was no reason for her to have stayed at home. He played golf all the morning, came home briefly to lunch, dozed in his chair after it and then accepted a telephoned invitation to join a foursome. He had made no comment on the fact that this was the day on which applicants might be expected to call in answer to the notices in the weekly newspaper; she felt certain that he had forgotten all about it. His apologies, as he hurried out of the house and into his car, were brief and absentminded.

She did not miss him. More and more she was finding happiness in the company of the twins. They were suspicious of any change in routine and needed to be reassured, but on the whole they were the most placid pair she had ever encountered, responsive, intelligent, and as laughter-loving as herself. She took them out for a brief airing before tea and then left them free to crawl in and out of the rooms while she prepared dinner for herself and Julian.

When they were in bed, she laid the table in the drawing room, checked the oven temperature and settled down to wait. But she was not waiting for applicants. When the telephone rang at ten minutes past eight, she picked up the receiver and heard what she had expected to hear.

"Natalie? Julian here. Look, I'm awfully sorry. I meant to ring earlier to tell you not to wait dinner for me. I'm at a restaurant in town — four of us are having a quick meal and then going on to an impromptu organ recital. I'd come and fetch you, but I know you can't leave the twins. Everything all right?"

"Yes."

"Don't wait up."

"I won't."

She put down the receiver, looked up the number of the hotel and dialed. She asked for Mr. Henry Downing.

He was not in his room. He was not in the restaurant. He was at last located in the bar.

"Downing here."

"This is Miss Trammers."

"Hatterley? No, Natalie. I remember now. You have two charming children."

"I've also got a nice dinner for two. My brother decided to eat out. Do you like chicken-and-mushroom pie?"

161

"Let me taste it, and I'll tell you."

"Can you extricate yourself from those women who were propping up the bar with you?"

"I'll do my best. See you."

He arrived in less than ten minutes. She had left the front door open for him; she heard it close behind him, and then he was in the kitchen. His arms were full of flowers. He laid them on a chair and took her into his arms.

She released herself without haste. He had a rather overconfident air for which she did not blame him; her telephone call must have sounded like the cry of a woman hungry for more than chicken-and-mushroom pie.

He picked up the flowers and handed them to her with a bow.

"For you, with my love. The stems are a bit wet. They're straight out of the hall vase of the hotel, fresh yesterday morning."

She put them into water.

"I don't suppose you want any more to drink," she said.

"Why not? I hadn't been in the bar all the evening."

"Then help yourself."

"As a matter of fact, I'd rather eat. I'm empty. I think your sudden summons might have upset my digestive processes; why, I ask myself, did she ask me to fill in, if she didn't like me?"

"It could be that she didn't like to see good chicken pie wasted."

"She could have heated it up for tomorrow.

Her only reason for asking me must have been because she wanted my company."

"Or any company."

"My company," he repeated. "Shall I go up and look at the twins?"

"No. You can carry in the soup, unless you're accident prone, like your aunt Clarice."

The telephone rang, and she answered. It was Mrs. Wray.

"Natalie? We're back. My husband wasn't feeling well, so there was no point in staying away. I've put him to bed; if he's not better in the morning, I'll ask the doctor to look in."

"I'm so sorry. Henry's here — would you like a word with him?"

"Oh, is he with you? I tried the hotel, but they said he was out."

Henry took the receiver. Natalie left him to talk and carried the soup to the table. He came in and reported.

"Both of them back, Marcus in bed with a temperature. She says she doesn't think it's anything serious."

They ate by candlelight. Henry began by outlining his day.

"Church this morning. I didn't see you there. You should have taken the twins; you can't start them too early on the right paths. I got there early, to see the school file in."

"I thought the school had a chapel of its own."

"It has. But on every first Sunday of the month they attend the town service. They even bring

163

their own choir along, which is a mistake because it doesn't blend with the town choir, which is composed of aged ladies with cracked voices, and corpulent tenors just off the note. I saw Leo coming in, and remembered being one of the long, long procession, all those years ago."

"Were you in the choir?"

"No. I've got a splendid voice, but unfortunately it's monotonal. I imagine I'm singing the tune, but what I'm actually doing is grinding out the same note all the time. Very off-putting for those to left and right of me. Tone-deaf, like my father. I suppose Leo's musical know-how comes from his mother."

"What's she like?"

"Slim, beautiful, elegant. Spoilt. Spoilt by her parents, by her uncles and aunts, by the servants and finally by my father. Oddly enough, that kind of lifelong pampering doesn't always produce regrettable results. People like my stepmother don't grow too demanding because their demands have always been, so to speak, anticipated. She's turned out surprisingly nice. The only serious obstacles she's ever run up against have been my father's insistence on Leo's being born at Downing and my insistence on his coming to school here. And spoilt or not, she's amusing. You'd like her. I'd spend more time in her house if she didn't fill it with a nonstop succession of visitors, most of them Italian, all of them overexcitable. Nobody talks; they all shout. I like to take it in small doses, and I think even Leo sometimes feels he could do with a bit less Latin exuberance. The Downing side of him disapproves of so much — what's the word? — extroversion. What relations have you got, apart from your two brothers?"

"No close ones. My mother quarrelled with most of them. She enjoyed what she called tiffs. Having a tiff meant taking the opportunity of telling somebody exactly what she thought of them. Then she was ready to make it up and was surprised to learn that she'd lost a friend — or a relation. She was a very good bridge player — she used to start clubs, and they went well until everybody began to quarrel."

"You always lived with her?"

"I always lived at home. She never liked the house much — it was too rambling, too formless. She went up to London when my father died and stayed there, trying to get Maurice and his wife to live with her or let her live with them. That didn't come off, so she came back — happier than when she went away because from then on she had a built-in complaint: her son's ingratitude."

She got up to make coffee; he carried in the tray, and she brought out Julian's cognac. They sat on the sofa, the tray beside them. He put out a hand and took one of hers, and she did not withdraw it.

Silence fell — easy and companionable. He watched the soft light on her face, the gleam of her hair. Shadows enclosed them. He would have liked to banish from his mind all thought of past or future; he wanted to enjoy to the full the happiness of this evening. But it was only the past he succeeded in excluding; more and more he found himself confronting the future. With feelings that were a mixture of surprise, apprehension and exaltation, he acknowledged to himself that he was in love. Seated beside her in the glow of the candles, he ceased to question or to resist. He loved her — deeply.

He would have given much to know her feelings for him. Summoning his resolution, he decided that this was perhaps the moment in which to ask.

"You were going to think over my proposition," he began. "Did you come to any conclusion?"

"You made me a proposition?"

"I suggested your dropping that other fellow, whoever he is, and taking me on instead."

"Before putting forward ideas like that, shouldn't you give yourself more time to consider?"

"Will you be serious, please? You know very well it was a well-weighed and well-considered decision."

"What was?"

"To marry you and settle down."

"When did you first weigh and consider?"

"When I gave you a lift from my aunt's house to this house, taking in Brighton on the way. I'd already had trouble getting you out of my mind after our first meeting. I love you and I'd like to marry you, and I'd like to know how the idea of marrying me strikes you. It would mean living in Downing forever."

"But —"

"But what?"

"Your work is —"

"Never mind about my work. Do you love me?"

"Do I have to answer that without weighing and considering?"

"Yes."

"Here and now?"

He drew her nearer.

"The way to find out for certain," he said, "is to keep quite still and close your eyes while I kiss you. The kiss lasts exactly ten seconds, and at the end of it you know, one way or the other. Ready?"

"Yes."

She leaned towards him — and then drew back. A car had come into the drive and stopped outside the window. Cold with rage and frustration, Henry heard the sound of a key being inserted in the front door.

"Julian," said Natalie.

"Why now, for God's sake? He can hardly have finished dinner."

The door opened. Julian stood on the threshold, his face pale, his eyes half closed. He looked blindly at Natalie, and she spoke with compassion.

167

"One of your migraines?"

"Yes. Sorry. Not feeling too good. I'll go up to bed, I think. Could you —"

She was on her feet.

"I'll bring you up a drink of hot lemon juice."

He turned towards the stairs.

"Came on about seven," he told her, "but I thought it might pass off. Had to come away from dinner."

He went upstairs, and Henry followed Natalie into the kitchen.

"Does he often get migraines?" he asked.

"I don't know how often he has them nowadays. He used to have them pretty frequently when he lived at home. Nobody ever succeeded in curing them."

"How long do they last?"

"Depends. He said this one started at seven. He'll take this hot lemon drink and a couple of aspirins and sleep it off. Then he'll come down and make tea and toast."

"Do you want me to go away?"

"Not unless you want to."

He did not want to, but he was aware that the evening was over. She had been warm and responsive. The atmosphere had been intimate, infinitely promising. Everything had pointed to a satisfying climax. A fine time, he told himself savagely, for Fate to introduce a migraine.

He did not linger. Soon after he had left, Julian came downstairs in a dressing gown and asked for tea. Natalie, putting away plates and dishes in the kitchen, pulled out a chair for him.

"Sit down. I'll make you tea and toast."

"No. Just tea. Sorry I broke up your party."

"No party. I invited Henry Downing to eat your dinner."

"I should have rung you earlier. The whole day's been a strain. I don't like discussing school affairs when I'm playing golf, as you know, but I got involved in plans to enter one of the orchestras in a national competition, and it went on through the afternoon and I felt my eyes going muzzy."

"Why don't you go up to bed and let me take up your tea?"

"No. It's a relief to be over it. I wish to God someone would find a cure. How many so-called cures have I tried out?"

"Some of them were old wives' remedies recommended by Mother's bridge cronies."

"Not all. I wasted a lot of money on self-styled specialists."

He drank several cups of tea and went back to bed. When she went up later, she stood at her window for a time, looking at the black, starless night. The sole gleam of light to be seen came from the house next door. It was the hall light, but it gave sufficient illumination to enable her to see that Mr. Wray's room was unoccupied.

She turned away and began to undress; the fact puzzled but did not interest her. She had a mental picture of Mrs. Wray tucking her husband up in her own bed and hovering over him with remedies. It would not be a new role for her — she had nursed her father for many years. How did the old saying go? For the young man, a mistress; for the older man, a hostess; for the old man, a nurse. Well, Mr. Wray had got his nurse.

Chapter

8

The next day was Monday, and Mrs. Lingford arrived on the stroke of nine. There had been no difficulty about transport; she had only to step into a bus outside her door, step out of it at the end of the lane and walk the few hundred yards to Julian's door. She was dressed, as on her previous visit, in unrelieved black. She let herself in, put her umbrella on the hall stand, hung up her coat and put on a black cotton overall, but did not remove her black woolen beret. Seeing Julian in the drawing room and Natalie in the kitchen with the twins, she opened a cupboard under the stairs, dragged out a vacuum cleaner and two dusters and went to work upstairs. She had given no response whatever to Julian's nod or Natalie's words of greeting. Throughout the following two and a half hours she remained dumb.

Her attitude towards the twins was one of extreme caution. If she had to pass them, she went in a wide circle, eyeing them warily. From time to time she stopped to gaze at them expressionlessly, like a not very intelligent visitor to a zoo. At eleven o'clock she made herself some tea, drank it standing and returned to work. At twenty-five minutes past eleven she took off her overall, rolled it into a bundle and pushed it into her canvas handbag, put on her coat, took her umbrella and departed.

Apart from Mrs. Lingford, the situation regarding domestic helpers seemed to have reached a stalemate. No applicants had appeared in response to the advertisement. Natalie hoped nobody would choose to appear when she was in the middle of her coaching sessions.

But when she had put the twins down for their afternoon rest, she heard a car stop outside the house. A few moments afterwards there was a peremptory knock on the front door. She went down and opened it, to see a tall, thin woman of middle age dressed in a smart tweed coat with a matching hat. At the gate a small car with two people in it waited.

"Good morning." The woman indicated the newspaper she was holding. "Could I speak to whoever it was who put an advertisement for a nanny into this paper?"

It was a harsh voice, and the request was made abruptly. Natalie resisted a strong impulse to close the door.

"I put it in," she said.

"Then I won't waste your time. I just came to find out whether it was for this house or elsewhere. You see, I've worked only in large establishments, and I couldn't take on a job unless there was a day and night nursery and my own bedroom and sitting room and bathroom. There's nothing of that kind here, unless the house is much bigger than it looks. Is it?"

"No."

"Then I'm afraid it's no use asking for any further particulars. I hope you'll find someone of the kind you want. Good-bye."

"Good-bye."

Natalie watched her fold herself up — it was a two-door car — and squeeze into the back. The car drove away, and she shut the door thankfully. She wouldn't hand the twins over to anybody with a voice like that. Wanted a job with royalty, obviously.

She looked at her watch: just over ten minutes before the history pupils appeared. Time to make herself a cup of coffee.

But as she reached the kitchen, there was another knock — this time timid. When she opened the door, she saw a man and a woman, both approaching middle age.

"We've come about the advert," the man said.

"Is the post taken?" the woman asked.

"No. Will you come in?"

They followed her to the dining room and seated themselves on the edge of two chairs, waiting to be interrogated. The woman looked at Natalie; the man examined his boots.

"Could I know your names?"

"Day. Mr. and Mrs. Day. I'm forty and my husband's forty-two, and we've been working for an old gentleman just outside Downing — Spode village. We were there for six years, just on. I was cook-housekeeper, and my husband was sort of a general worker, waiting at table when there was guests, seeing to the old gen-

173

tleman, doing a bit in the garden, keeping the fires going, that kind of thing. Then the old gentleman died — three months ago all but two days — and we took a job as married couple in London. But we couldn't settle. We weren't used to city life, and we wanted to get back to this part of the world. We feel at home here, being born in Spode, both of us. We've got good references — I brought them with me. The old gentleman left us a little bit of money, and what we said was that we'd take it easy looking for a job, not be in a hurry, take our time and find somewhere we liked and where we could be happy."

"That's right," corroborated Mr. Day.

"What exactly was the job here, if I may ask, miss?"

Natalie told them. The idea of a mother deserting her children made Mr. Day's rather bulging eyes bulge still further. He made clicking noises to show his disapproval.

"Unnatural," he said.

"Perhaps the first thing," Natalie suggested, "would be to look over the house."

She led them over it. They murmured their approval of the spacious rooms, the automatic heating, the wide windows, the polished parquet. They crept into the twins' bedroom and looked with unfeigned pleasure and admiration at the two sleeping forms.

"Lovely children," Mrs. Day whispered.

"The little boy was a bit subdued this

morning," Natalie told them on the way down-stairs. "I wondered if he had a tooth coming."

"His back ones'll be due," Mrs. Day said. "They can be nasty when they're coming through. I used to give my baby a nice bone to chew. Not chicken bones — they chip. A nice hard bone like a chop bone."

"I'll try it," Natalie said gratefully.

They had returned to the dining room. Mrs. Day spoke hesitatingly.

"The house is lovely, miss. But there's just one thing . . ."

She paused, and her husband spoke.

"You've got to tell her," he pointed out. "She's got to know, hasn't she?"

"Yes. Well, it's like this, miss. We . . ."

"We're good workers," Mr. Day said firmly. "We're a bit old-fashioned, I suppose; we like work. We'd give you every satisfaction. But the truth is, there's a snag, miss. It didn't matter with the old gentleman — we had our own quarters and there was a lot of room and we could keep Frankie with us. Frankie's our little boy. Seven, he is, and never a mite of trouble all the years we were with the old gentleman. But when we went to work in London, there was no room for him. At first we thought we wouldn't take the job be-cause of that, but the people were nice, and the job was well paid, so we thought we'd try leaving Frankie with his aunt — my wife's sister. She was very fond of Frankie, and he liked her, and she had no children of her own and looked for-

175

ward to having him living with her. But he didn't settle. She didn't tell us anything until we'd given up the job and gone back to Spode — and then it all came out. The police had been round."

"Police?"

"Yes, miss. He'd been setting fire to things. He tried to burn his kindergarten down. The doctor said he would have been all right if he'd been with us."

"So whoever has us," summed up Mrs. Day, "has to have Frankie, too. A nicer little boy you couldn't meet anywhere, and not a bit of trouble since he was back with us — but he's big enough now to need a room of his own, miss, and I don't see where you could put him in this house."

Natalie was unable to make any suggestions. She sat silent and despondent. Something about the couple appealed to her. They were more than old-fashioned; they were out of date. The problem of Frankie apart, she knew that they would be willing and probably efficient workers. But there was no room for Frankie, and if there had been, she would have hesitated before putting a pyromaniac into it.

"I'm sorry," she said at last. "I think you would have suited very well — but I'm afraid there's only the one spare room upstairs. I can't offer you the room at the back of this one be-cause it's used as a study."

There seemed nothing more to say. Mrs. Day groped in her handbag and produced a sheet of paper.

"That's our name and address, miss. If you hear of anyone else needing a couple, perhaps you'd let us know."

"I will. I'm so sorry."

"Not your fault, miss," Mr. Day said stoically. "The house is just a bit too small, that's all. Good day, miss. Thank you." They got into their small car — she thought they might have bought it with the money they had inherited from the old gentleman. The school car drove in as they drove out.

Henry arrived to take Leo back to school after his lesson. He returned to ask for news.

"Nothing hopeful," she told him. "A nanny who was too grand to take the job, and a married couple who would have done nicely if they hadn't had a son who's given to setting fire to things, including his school."

She broke off to go to the door and admit Mrs. Wray.

"I saw Henry's car and came in to tell you that I think Marcus is a little better. His temperature's down, but I'm going to keep him in bed. He says he's always been liable to these sudden attacks, but he's usually all right next morning. Natalie, have you had any luck with domestic help?"

Natalie gave her a summary of the situation.

"This Frankie — did they bring him?" Mrs. Wray asked.

"No."

"It's a pity you couldn't have seen him. They

177

sound a nice couple, and you could have recommended them, but not without knowing more of this young fire raiser. It sounds as though it was brought on by being separated too suddenly from his parents. All the same, he might go on being subject to outbreaks. Did they leave their address?"

"Yes. They live in Spode."

"Then I can easily find out more details. How is the coaching going?"

"Quite well, I think."

"I hear Leo's made friends with a little African boy whose father is in prison."

"Joshua's father — in prison!" Natalie said in dismay.

"In Africa," Henry said. "He made the mistake of criticizing the government."

"So I heard. Which government, I didn't gather," Mrs. Wray said. "As soon as I get my tongue round the name of one black ruler, he vanishes, and I have to try to pronounce the name of his successor. It's an odd world, isn't it? Your generation has had to come to terms with it, but it looks to me as though we're ruled by strikers and students. I try very hard to make myself believe that freedom's wonderful, democracy's the only hope, the submerged faces must be made to rise and rule, long live us all. But it's no use. I have nightmares about the world rushing rapidly to self-destruction. I wish I had what they call an objective outlook. I see everything too close."

"So does Natalie," Henry told her.

"Well, fight it, Natalie. Fight it. Why did you let me get on to world problems? We were talking about Joshua. There's no mother, is there?"

"No," Julian answered. "The headmaster's going to make arrangements for him to stay in England for the holidays."

"Good." Mrs. Wray went to the door. "I must get back to Marcus. About Frankie: I'll ring Mrs. Whitestone; she knows a lot about the people in Spode."

Henry walked with her to her gate. Natalie got the twins out of bed and began the preparations for tea. Miss Drew telephoned to confirm her Friday visit.

Mrs. Whitestone arrived as they were finishing tea, skipping agilely out of a long-nosed car and running energetically up the steps.

"Just popped in for a minute," she said. "Got a call from Henry's aunt about some people from Spode. First of all, let me take a look at the twins."

The twins, still at tea, listened politely to her flattering comments on their beauty and bloom. Randall made a speech in reply.

"They're pets. They're about the only children I've seen who make me wish I'd had some of my own," she declared. "No, no tea, thanks. Can't stop. I only want to say that I know all about this little boy Frankie. You can recommend the Days to anybody without the slightest qualm. In fact, I shall go round myself telling people that they're available. Frankie is all right. They shouldn't have left him alone with that aunt. She's not a bad woman, but she's not used to children, and she fussed him. He was used to being on his own, and he rebelled, that's all. It's tragic, Natalie, that you hadn't room in this house for the three of them. All your problems would have been solved. A nanny for the twins wouldn't have been difficult to find once you had people working in the house. However, we can't build another room, so we'll have to wait and see who else turns up. Henry, I ran into your two aunts in town, and they told me you'd met Blanche's husband. You didn't speak to him?"

"No."

"You told them you thought he looked scholarly — that'll appeal to my husband."

"Did I say scholarly?" Henry thought it over. "Yes, I suppose he does. But I'd also say that he looked rather frail."

"Frail? You mean delicate?"

"Yes. I hope for Aunt Blanche's sake that he's stronger than he gives the impression of being."

"I hope so, too," Mrs. Whitestone said fervently. "I've never seen her so happy. It would be awful if it didn't last. Where did you see him?"

"It was quite by chance. I was going in — he was coming out."

"Of the hotel?"

"Yes. I recognized him from the photograph she's got in her room."

"Well, I hope you're wrong about his health." She turned to Natalie. "What do you think of Miss Drew?"

Natalie hesitated.

"She's very efficient. But I suppose you could call her a bit bossy," she said at last.

"You could indeed," Mrs. Whitestone agreed. "I'm afraid that manner of hers has lost her a good many friends in this town. You mustn't let her impose on you. And you must remember not to leave any food about — she's got a gargantuan appetite. Put out her meal, and lock up everything else. Good-bye, my dear. Good-bye, Henry. I hope you're making yourself useful and not just hanging about and getting in Natalie's way. Natalie, I hope you have good luck with the next lot of applicants."

Back in the kitchen after her departure, Natalie spoke despondently.

"Next lot? I don't suppose there'll be a next lot," she said.

Henry took one of her hands and rubbed it against his cheek.

"You're not getting pessimistic?" he asked.

"No. I'm just losing hope, that's all. I think I'm here forever. Do you really think your aunt's husband looks delicate?"

"Never mind about my aunt's husband. Let's discuss your staying here forever. That's what I was talking to you about when your brother staged a migraine. Could we go on from where he came in?"

"I don't need to count ten. And I wouldn't dream of closing my eyes. I'm going to keep them wide open in the future."

"Say after me: 'I love you, and I'll marry you, for better or for worse.' "

"I love you, and I'll marry you when I've got Julian settled, which may be never."

He took her into his arms, and she leaned against him with the happy recollection that getting Julian settled would now be as much in his interest as in hers.

"If you'd married that other fellow, would you have lived in Brighton?"

"No. Edinburgh."

"Terribly cold winds up there. You've had a lucky escape. Could we sit down and plan a lovely future for us both?"

She freed herself.

"No. I've got to go into town."

"Why?"

"I need bones."

"Bones?"

"Chop bones for teething twins. It was Mrs. Day's idea, and I like it."

"They're teething?"

"I think Randall's showing signs. They're both going to have a nice, well-cooked chop bone with their supper. Are you coming with me, or are you going back to the hotel?"

"I'm going with you. We'll go in my car. Let's put the twins in."

"Are you sure you want to come?"

"Wherever you go, I'm going with you. I don't know where the ends of the earth are — how can there be ends to something circular? — but if you're going there, I'm going too."

"The object at the moment is the Regent Lane butcher."

"The shops shut at five thirty. That includes the butcher. It's now five thirty-three."

"Damn."

"So you'll have to follow me."

"Where to?"

"The hotel. I have a great pull with the chef. We shall accost him and demand chops for teething twins."

"You really think you can —"

"I can. Ask me for anything you want; my answer will always be the same: I can. Can I give up my freedom without regret in order to make you my wife? I can. Can I support you adequately? I can. Can I devote the rest of my life to you, selflessly, devotedly and also unswervingly? I can, I can, I can. Where are the twins' coats?"

"In the hall."

"Then come on. I'll take the girl one. You take the brother."

Chapter

9

With the departure of the Days, no further applicants appeared to fill the vacant posts. There was only Mrs. Lingford — but Natalie was beginning to feel that she was worth three of any ordinary worker.

She was still totally unresponsive in regard to Julian and Natalie, but her silence did not extend to machines. She muttered fiercely at the dusters, the mops and brooms, the vacuum cleaner. Her grudges against life, whatever they were, were vented on the household implements, and one by one they gave way under the strain. Dusters tore; mops shed their curls; the vacuum cleaner cast off its long, snakelike tube. She bore away the wounded and brought them back next day, mended, Natalie presumed, by the bachelor brother with whom she shared a modest villa. She judged him to be a good handyman, for the things came back in better condition than they had been before Mrs. Lingford's onslaughts. Back in service, they were again thrashed and beaten and slapped. The furniture, which had never had its fill of polishing, now shone. The floors gleamed. Cobwebs, which had hung undisturbed in remote corners, were attacked with such savagery that they came away with flakes of plaster adhering to them. The request to leave Julia's things untouched had from the first been ignored; his mattress was regularly turned and aired, his curtains taken down and shaken, his cupboards emptied, the shelves scrubbed and the contents artistically rearranged.

In time Natalie had come to follow Randall's example and made audible comments on the situation. He made long speeches of congratulation; she made brief ones. Mrs Lingford took not the slightest notice of either, but Mrs. Gilling rang up one afternoon to report that the bachelor brother had told the postman, who had told the butcher, who had told Mrs. Gilling that Mrs. Lingford had expressed unqualified approval of the house, the twins and Natalie herself. Julian was not mentioned — probably because he had made audible comments regarding employees who exceeded their duties and disturbed people's personal arrangements.

An unexpected telephone call came one evening from Freddie. She asked brusquely when Natalie was planning to return to Brighton. Natalie informed her that there was at present no prospect of this.

"You can't stay there forever!" Freddie protested. "If you can't find anybody in Downing, let me try London."

"Julian says they used to try London. Nobody from London would stay here."

"I don't blame them. But I'll go along to some

agencies and see what I can do. Are you doing all the searching, or is Julian making some kind of effort?"

"He's got his job; he hasn't much time."

"Didn't I tell you? You're stuck. You know that Michael Morley's due back in less than a month?"

"Yes."

"Has he been in touch with you."

"Yes."

"I can't think what's the matter with you. You don't sound in the least worried about the situation."

"How does worrying help?"

"It keeps you looking for people. I know you'll let this drift on, just as Julian's letting it drift on. That kind of attitude is catching. I'm going to see what the London agencies can do. If Julian has to pay twice as much, it serves him right."

Catching? Perhaps, Natalie acknowledged at the end of the call. She did not think she was drifting, but she had certainly become resigned to waiting.

And in the meantime, with Mrs. Lingford to take care of the housework, she had more leisure. She found time, now, to invent games to play with the twins. She drove them to the park and put them on the swings. They fed the swans on the miniature lake. She explored the countryside, the twins alert and observant in their new, brightly coloured winter outfits. She took advantage of Miss Drew's visits to go see the controversial films at the local cinema. And wherever she went, with or without the twins, Henry Downing went, too.

His greatest usefulness, she told him, was his daily morning visit to his house to build a great fire to warm the hall. This was their retreat, their protection from the increasingly inclement weather, the twins' playground on rainy days. It was a restaurant at which they ate simple lunches or teas. It was a haven in which they stayed contentedly while Mrs. Gilling and Freddie went on searching for domestic treasures.

Natalie was always in the house when Julian returned in the evenings. The twins were tucked up in bed, the oven warming for the take-away dinners, herself ready to listen to his comments on the day. He did not appear interested to learn how she was spending her time. This might be a strange life, she sometimes paused to reflect, but strange or not, she was enjoying it.

"And why not?" Henry argued. "Why not enjoy it? You've got everything to make you happy: me, the twins and someone to do the housework."

He got up to throw a massive log onto the fire. He and Natalie were finishing their after-lunch coffee in the hall of his house. The twins were playing with the chessmen, setting them out — upright or recumbent — on the chessboard and pushing them to and fro. It was a Tuesday afternoon, the beginning of the third week of what Freddie had called drifting.

"Have you noticed" — Henry poured more

coffee into their cups — "how helpful Fate has been in furthering my cause?"

"You have a cause?"

"Yes. Pursuing you. Look at the way Fate worked on my behalf."

"As how?"

"First, by bringing you to Downing, Second, by keeping you here. Third, for having kept me free from previous entanglements, and you almost free. Fourth, by leading me to the final decision to keep this house. Which reminds me that we've got a problem to solve."

She turned to look at him.

"A new one?"

"The Christmas holiday problem."

"Isn't Joshua going to Italy with Leo?"

"It doesn't look like it. Leo's developed a kind of protective instinct over the affair. Some devil told him, or maybe he overheard somewhere, that prisoners in those dark continents have a way of going into custody and not coming out again. And Joshua had been told by his relations that going to Africa was for the moment out of the question — which was why he accepted Leo's invitation to go to Italy. But there are complications. The headmaster had a talk with me last night and told me that five — one, two, three, four, five — of Joshua's relations from various parts of England are converging on Downing for the Christmas holidays. They've booked a room at the hotel."

"*One* room?"

188

"One. Three in the bed and two under it, I presume. The headmaster said it would be unthinkable to take Joshua away — and I agreed. I drove to the school and talked to Leo. He said firmly — and I know that tone — that in that case he would prefer to spend the Christmas holidays here. With me. And of course, Joshua. He said he saw no reason why we couldn't live in this house."

"And Leo's mother?"

"I rang her late last night. She'd arranged everything at her house — and skiing at her chalet after Christmas. Friends had been invited. So she was not pleased at the change of plan."

"Was she angry with Leo?"

"No. With me. And to a lesser degree with my aunts. She thinks we've been in league to turn him into a Downing. She must think we worked fast."

"So you've got two boys to look after during the holidays. Why not book them in at the hotel?"

"Not a chance. Leo wouldn't hear of it. We're to be here. That means fixing up two bedrooms — one for them, one for me. It means stocking up with food. Fuel's no problem."

"It means cooking for them and seeing to their laundry."

"We'll manage. There'll be the two of them, and you and me."

"I'll be here?"

"On and off. If you've got a staff for your

brother by then, you're invited to occupy a third bedroom here. If no staff, we hope you'll spend all your spare time with us. Snow sports. I'll make a sled — I used to toboggan down the slope behind the lake. I once made a snowman so high that I had to climb a tree to put his hat on and his pipe in his mouth. There used to be some brass warming pans around this house; I'll look for them."

"I didn't bring any winter clothes with me. I didn't anticipate spending Christmas here."

"No problem. You buy a complete new outfit, like the twins. If you haven't enough money, I'll advance it. I'm rather rich — did I tell you that?"

"No."

"I was keeping it up my sleeve as a last inducement. But to return to what I was saying, Fate has done its best for me. Especially by removing that fellow, I've forgotten his name, to distant parts. Let's hope he stays there."

"He's on his way back."

"Is he planning to see you?"

"I suppose so."

"Write and tell him I forbid it. Where did you meet him?"

"In London. He was one of Maurice's friends."

And it was Maurice, she remembered, who had decided that here was the husband that he and Freddie would welcome. Maurice it was who had nudged on the affair persistently and, he thought, unobtrusively. His efforts had resulted in making her decide that — for what it was worth — she liked Michael Morley better than the other men she knew. But she had never reached the point of imagining herself in love with him, and she had given him little or no encouragement. Before he left England, she had firmly refused to marry him, but his letters, frequent and undiscouraged, merely stated that he was confident of making her change her mind when he returned.

She got up and walked over to the twins to rescue the chessmen, who were now being chewed. Henry, staring into the fire, gave himself up to dreams. Fate had indeed been kind, he mused. She had been held prisoner, thus giving him time and opportunity to plead his cause. He was not vain enough to believe that if he had been in open competition, he would have awakened in her any response.

She began to get the twins ready for the road. He went across and took their coats from her.

"Not yet." He put the coats on a chair. "We've got a little more time. Come back to the fire."

In the firelight she studied him with a puzzled frown.

"What I find hard to believe," she said, "is that I've known you hardly any time. And I hardly know you."

"You know I love you. And you love me."

"Yes, but —"

"But?"

"You can't say we know much about each other, can you?"

"There's a lot of future in which you can fill in details like whether I'm a stable character or whether I've any criminal tendencies or whether I'll prove a faithful husband. You'll learn as time goes on. How could people ever marry if they waited to uncover all the unknown factors? We love one another — that's enough for the moment."

"What do you mean by love?"

"Wanting to be with you. Wanting to stay with you. What's your definition?"

"Thinking about you most of the time, first thing when I wake up and last thing when I'm falling asleep. Being with you seems natural. Having to do without you seems . . . well, unthinkable. Is that love?"

"It'll do."

Sometime later they remembered the twins' coats and put them on the children.

"I forgot to tell you that Clarice and Geraldine want to see them. Can you drop in there on your way home? I'll meet you there, and we won't stay long," Henry said.

On arrival at the hotel annex the twins were not subjected to any excess of attention. Their hostesses pronounced them to be fine babies, shook each of them by the hand and made them comfortable on the sofa.

"It's nice to see you again," Geraldine told Natalie. "We stop Mrs. Gilling every time we see her, to ask how the staff problem is getting on. Sit down over there, won't you? I suppose it's too late to offer you tea?"

"Too late for tea, but not too late for biscuits for the twins," Clarice said, getting some out of a tin. "Henry, we ran into a friend of yours today — Mrs. Thorley. Do you remember that rather pretty woman you used to —"

"No," said Henry. "Is that the little pot of azaleas I brought you? It seems to be doing very well."

"It's beautiful. Mrs. Thorley was with her sister. Was it the sister you liked, or was it —"

"I can't remember."

"You should. You were very friendly with her, whichever she was. She told me that she had divorced her husband. It seems to take no time at all these days, and certainly no trouble. Do you remember, Geraldine, how difficult it used to be for women — like poor Lady Ricks, for example — to get rid of the dreadful husbands they were saddled with?"

"That's one of the things that's better than it used to be in our time," Geraldine said. "That and clothes. So much more colourful, so much more comfortable these days. And food, so much less elaborate, none of those complicated dishes that people had to serve when they gave dinner parties. I must say there isn't a great deal that I regret about those old days. And I'm so enjoying living here in the town, so close to all our friends, so easy to drop in and have little chats."

Natalie was brushing biscuit crumbs off the twins. She said it was time to take them home.

"Oh, such a short visit!" Geraldine exclaimed. "But I won't keep you because I know it's the babies' bedtime. Henry, you got away last time without giving me your contribution to the refugee fund. Have you got your checkbook with you?"

Henry said, somewhat reluctantly, that he had.

"Then sit down here, dear boy, and write me a large check. Don't be stingy with the noughts. Who knows? You might win the big prize. Have you seen any of our posters in the shops in town?"

"No."

Clarice brought one to show him. It was a highly coloured display depicting a Christmas hamper filled with seasonal delicacies. A dead turkey dangled from one corner, a dead duck from another. There were tins of mince pies, plum pudding, biscuits, tea, coffee, liqueur chocolates.

"Clarice designed the poster. This hamper," Geraldine explained to Natalie, "is something my sister and I offer every year to those who contribute to whatever charity we happen to have been collecting for. This year it has been the refugee fund. The hamper is filled for us by various shops in the town — all gifts, of course — and towards Christmas, we invite all those who have contributed to the refugee fund to come to the house of the oldest inhabitant, whoever that proves to be. We put all the numbers into a bag, and the oldest inhabitant draws out the winning number, and the winner gets the hamper. All this organization is, of course, hard work for us, but we never refuse to undertake it. Now you and Henry will be given your numbers — you are going to contribute to the fund, aren't you?"

Natalie, mesmerized, groped in her bag and produced some money. Clarice opened a large book with lined pages on which were numbers and, against the numbers, names.

"So far, eight hundred and seventy contributors," said Clarice.

"The last time I saw the bank manager," said Geraldine, "he told me he'd got over two thousand pounds. That's just over last year's total."

She tore off a small square of paper on which was printed the number 871. This she handed to Henry. Natalie was given number 872. Their contributions were put into an envelope, and Henry was asked to drop it into the bank night safe on his way home.

"You'll get your receipts from the bank," she explained. "I don't keep any money here. Thank you both for helping the fund. I hope one of you will win the Christmas hamper. You'll need it, Henry, if you're going to look after two boys throughout the holidays."

"I didn't think that item of news had got round yet," Henry told her.

"I heard it from the headmaster two hours

ago. Even if he'd said nothing, I would have been able to put two and two together. I know that Leo is very friendly with that little African boy, and the hotel people told me that his relations were booked into the hotel. But they said you hadn't booked for yourself and Leo."

"No. I'm thinking of staying up at the house."

Both his aunts looked at him in astonishment.

"But, my dear boy," Geraldine pointed out, "the place is almost denuded of furniture. And it's unheated. And you insisted on our taking away most of the linen."

"No stores, nothing to eat or drink," Clarice added.

"We'll manage," Henry said.

"Well, if you do decide to use the house, you must let us know, and we'll take you up some things."

Henry, leaving this offer in the air, followed Natalie out to the cars and settled the twins beside her. He asked if she was thinking of dropping in to see Mrs. Wray, and she said that she was not. On the way home, however, she pondered on the fact that there had never been any repetition of Mrs. Wray's early assurance that she would be glad to see her anytime she cared to go in. Perhaps the newly married, she thought, however mature, liked to keep themselves to themselves for a time. She knew from Henry that the couple had refused many invitations to lunch or dine out.

But Mrs. Wray, coming in for a moment after

dinner, had a more disquieting explanation to give for this lack of social activity.

"Marcus hasn't been well," she told Natalie and Julian. "I'm worried about him — but I don't like to say so. Men hate being fussed. I learned that when I looked after my father."

"Have you asked a doctor to look at him?" Julian asked.

"No. He's got his own doctor in London, and he said if it was necessary — which he won't admit — he'd go up and see him. If I could get him to rest, I think he'd be all right, but he never leaves his desk. I persuaded him to have a little dinner, but back he went, and he's at it now, writing out notes." She turned to Natalie. "The headmaster told me that Leo's enjoying his lessons with you. But I forgot to ask if he had joined the choir."

"Yes, he joined," Julian said. "He was wavering, but when he heard that we're to have a candlelit carol service, he gave in. Look, I'm sorry — I haven't offered you a drink."

"I don't want anything, thanks. I've got to get back. Marcus is probably wandering round the house in his dressing gown. I don't want him to catch cold."

Julian went with her to her gate. Natalie went upstairs, looked at the twins and then went into her room and closed the door. Before putting on the light, she walked to the window to take her usual glance at the night. It was cloudy, but there was a moon which gave the fields a frosty

197

glimmer. Next door she could see an empty desk, an unused bed and a dressing gown hanging on the bed rail. Mr. Wray must have finished his notes.

Julian came upstairs, knocked on her door, opened it and asked apprehensively if any further arrangements had been made with Miss Drew.

"Only the usual. She's coming on her free afternoon."

"From what I've heard here and there, you're about the only person who's been able to put up with her for as long as this."

"The twins like her, and she looks after them well. That's all that matters."

"You haven't arranged to give her any more dinners, I trust?"

"No."

"Glad to hear it. Good night."

Chapter

10

On returning to the house at half past six on Friday, Natalie found that Miss Drew had not made her usual preparations for departure.

"You're early, aren't you?" she asked Natalie.

"Only a few minutes. I didn't want to keep you waiting. Besides, I owe you some money. We didn't settle up last week." Miss Drew took the money that was owing and put it into her purse before saying that there was no need to pay her anything; she was perfectly willing to come for nothing.

"You didn't have to hurry back on my account," she added. "I've got a free evening. I was just going to settle down to clean one or two bits of silver."

"Please don't bother. Thank you for coming."

"Sure you wouldn't like me to stay on? I haven't a thing to do, so just ask. I gave that room at the back, that study, a good going-over."

Natalie frowned.

"You didn't touch any of the papers, I hope."

"I didn't throw any away, if that's what you mean. But mess! I never saw anything like it. Music books all over the place, sheets of paper with music on them, like I said, mess. I can't think what that cleaning woman does every morning. Mess is something I can't stand. Did you notice last time that I'd given your cupboard a going-over?"

"Yes. I'd really rather you didn't."

"It's no trouble. I like work. I'll help you get the dinner, if you like."

Compassion stirred in Natalie. It was dark, and the rain was pouring down; this was no evening to turn a cyclist into the street. But she knew that if she issued an invitation to dinner tonight, Miss Drew would turn the single occasion into a weekly habit.

"I won't keep you. Thanks all the same," she said.

Slowly, reluctantly, Miss Drew went into the hall and took down her leather jacket. Natalie felt her resolution weakening. Julian would be furious, but there was no point in giving way to him on all matters. He was spoiled enough.

She was opening her mouth to ask Miss Drew to stay when there was a puttering sound in the lane, followed by a three-note blast on a horn. Miss Drew stared wildly at Natalie and then gave a shout.

"It's the squire! That's his signal! It's him!"

She bounded to the door and flung it open. Pushing a motorbike into the drive was a large, burly man. It was not possible to see his features, as they were hidden beneath a scarlet helmet, but Miss Drew, in no doubt as to his identity, had plunged down the steps, uttering cries of welcome.

"Well, you old surprise packet, you! Fancy turning up without a word! Don't tell me you've been travelling in this weather. Here, gimme your bike."

He relinquished it, came up the steps and removed his helmet, revealing a ruddy, bearded countenance — more sailor than farmer, Natalie thought. Miss Drew, having propped the motorbike against the wall, took the steps in two bounds and performed an introduction.

"This is the squire. I've told you about him, haven't I? Look at him, wet and dripping and as cold as Christmas. Come in here, squire, and get that wet coat off you."

She led him to the drawing room and fussed round him, helping him take off his leather coat and plastic thigh boots, whipping out a handkerchief to wipe the raindrops off his face and plying him with questions.

"Why didn't you give me a ring to say you were coming? How's Mum and the others? Dad all right? Nothing wrong, is there, you coming up here suddenly like this?"

He turned a cheerful grin on Natalie.

"Talks all the time, she does," he apologized. "Sorry to bring in mud. It's been a dirty trip."

"And cold, too. You're frozen," Miss Drew told him. "Here, get closer to this radiator."

She pushed forward a comfortable chair and settled him in it. She draped his wet coat on the back of a smaller chair, put his helmet on the table and his gloves on the radiator to dry.

"Go on, give me all the news," she urged. "If you'd come five minutes later, I'd have been gone. How did you know where I was?"

"I went to the school. They told me."

Their combined weights, Natalie thought, watching them, must be somewhere round half a ton. And most of it solid muscle. Miss Drew had settled on the arm of the squire's chair and was embarking on another series of questions. There should be some offer of refreshment — tea, or something stronger? Tea would mean a long session, with Julian probably coming in in the middle of it.

Miss Drew solved the problem.

"Look, I know what'll warm you — a nice drop of something." She was at the cupboard. "You don't mind if I give him just half an inch of this, do you, Miss Travers?"

This was Julian's most expensive, most cherished brandy. The half inch deepened to two inches. Miss Drew placed the bottle on the table, ready for further use, and handed the glass to the squire.

"Go on, get that down you," she urged.

He took a sip, experimentally, and then a second with relish. At the third, he gave a long sigh of contentment, stretched out his legs and loosened the buttons of his woolen waistcoat.

"Just what I needed," he said. "Cold trip, like I told you. I had to come up to London on a bit of business, and I thought to myself while I'm halfway here, why don't I stretch it a bit and look

202

in on Millie? Just as I got out of London, it started coming down, and it hasn't stopped since, but I thought as I was on my way, I might as well keep going."

"You shouldn't have," Miss Drew said reproachfully. "You should've stopped and got into shelter. You know you're liable to catch cold. How long are you going to stay here?"

"Stay?" The squire was astounded. "I can't stay, woman. I've got a farm waiting for me."

"Not even for one night?" Miss Drew asked in dismay.

"Not even for half a night. After I've had a bit of grub I'm going to start back. I'll stay with my cousin Ben in Wimbledon and then get off first thing in the morning, back home."

While he was speaking, Natalie heard Julian's key in the front door. Miss Drew and the squire were too engrossed in one another to notice the sound of his arrival.

Julian went first to the kitchen with the take-away meal he had brought for dinner. Then he went to the drawing room, opened the door and came face to face with Natalie.

"Motorbike outside," he said. "Who —"

He stopped. For a few moments his astonished gaze went round the room, taking in the half-reclining figure of the squire, the coat drying on the back of a chair, the helmet on the table, the gloves on the radiator. The bottle of brandy, Natalie noted with relief, was out of sight. He mumbled something that might have been greeting or apology and retreated to the hall.

"Hey, don't go," Miss Drew called. "Come and meet the squire."

But Julian was on his way to his study. The door closed behind him, and the squire, who had risen, sat down again.

"There's one thing about being a farmer," he said. "You leave your work outside. I wouldn't —"

He was interrupted by a wild cry from the study. A moment later Julian appeared at the drawing room door, looking distraught and waving a sheaf of papers at Miss Drew.

"You've been in there." Fury made articulation difficult. "You were told to keep out, remember? But you went in."

"I gave the room a going-over, yes," admitted Miss Drew. "It needed it. It was —"

"Do you know how long it took me to arrange these papers? Hours. Hours and hours. I sat there last night getting them all straight, ready for the classes. You've wrecked all my preparations. Who asked you to go in there and mess up everything?"

"I should think you'd be grateful for —"

"And my bedroom, too. I told you to stay out of it, didn't I? But you didn't. If I could have found the key, I would have locked it, but —"

"Hey, look." The squire was on his feet, his face dark with anger. "You can't talk to my fiancée like that." He turned to Miss Drew.

"And what's this about bedrooms?"

"If you'll all listen to me for a moment —" Natalie began.

Julian broke in, his voice cold.

"You let her in in the first place," he said. "I told you she was to keep out of my bedroom, but she didn't. Now she's messed up my music. And she's brought her men friends here, as I told you she would. But you —"

"That's it." The squire spoke grimly. "That's the lot. Come on, Millie — we're moving."

"But —"

"Come on, I said. We're going. For good."

In a heavy silence the squire put on his coat and picked up his helmet and gloves. He and Miss Drew went into the hall; Miss Drew's bicycle was taken down the steps. She rode away, and the squire, still without a word, got onto his motorbike, and followed her. The sounds died away; Natalie closed the front door and joined Julian in the drawing room.

"Exit Miss Drew," she said.

"Thank God for that. I warned you. You can't say you took her on without knowing what she was like."

"I was grateful to be able to leave the twins with her. Where are you going?"

"Out. There's dinner for you on the kitchen table. I feel like getting out and forgetting what that study looked like. I'll have to re-sort all those papers."

Left alone, she thought of ringing Henry but

remembered that he was dining with the head-master and his wife. It was just as well, she decided; the dinner she had intended to offer him proved to be a tired-looking mixture of rice and fish which she did not think he would have relished. She warmed it, ate some and put the remainder into the refrigerator. Mrs. Lingford would take it home on Monday for her chickens.

She was thinking of going up to bed when the telephone rang.

"Is Julian there?" she heard Henry ask.

"No."

"I thought not. I passed what I thought was his car outside the Chinese restaurant. I'll be round in a minute."

"I thought you were dining with the head-master."

"I was. It's after eleven. I left. It was an eventful dinner — wait till I tell you."

He told her on his arrival. Six of them, he said, had sat down to dinner. The meal was interrupted by an urgent message from Miss Drew.

"Do you want all the dramatic details," he paused to ask, "or just the gist?"

"The gist."

"Well, the headmaster went into his study and was confronted by her and her fiancé, both of them breathing fire. She'd been insulted by a member of the school staff. Nobody had ever spoken to her like that, and nobody was ever going to be allowed to speak to her like that again. She was leaving, and at once. She would have stayed to work out her notice, but her fiancé insisted on taking her back with him now. There were people, he said, crying out for her services down in Devon. She could have six jobs tomorrow if she wanted them — jobs with people who knew how a gentleman should treat a lady."

"She went?"

"On the back of the motorbike. To the hotel for the night, to Devon in the morning. Her bike and her luggage are to be put on the train. She was paid in full, and nothing was said about her having to stay until the end of her contract."

"So the school's a matron short."

"For the moment. The headmaster's sorry she's gone because she was a good matron. He's glad she's gone because she was a difficult character and she was losing friends fast. The only real gap she's left is the twin-sitting one. You'll have to find someone else."

"Yes." Her tone was absent. "I suppose I must."

"Got anybody in mind?"

"Nothing definite."

"Then let's get comfortable and talk about ourselves." He pushed the sofa closer to the radiator, borrowed some extra cushions from neighbouring chairs and waved her to them. "Could I help us both to a drink?"

"Not me. You. There might be some brandy left, but Miss Drew used a lot of it to warm up her fiancé when he arrived."

"What was the row about?"

"She tidied his study. He'd got all his papers ready for this competition, and —"

"— she tidied those, too?"

"Yes."

"He seems to me to be a fellow who lives on his nerves."

"He lives on his music. If nothing gets in the way, he's calm and not in the least temperamental. But he loathed Miss Drew from the start."

"I'm happy to tell you that you won't have any trouble with my temperament. I'm — will you stop fidgeting? I'm trying to get my arms round you."

She got up and stood at the head of the sofa.

"Just a minute," she said. "I've got something to tell you."

He stretched himself full length, arms behind his head.

"Go ahead. I'm listening."

"It's something I've known . . . well, not known, exactly, just known without acknowledging it, for a long time. Almost as long as I've been here."

She paused, and he prompted her.

"Well, proceed."

"I'm trying. But I don't know how you're going to feel about it."

"Why don't you let me tell you what you're trying to tell me? Half a dozen words will do it: You want to keep the twins."

She stood gazing at him, not in surprise, but in an attempt to read his expression. He had spoken lightly, but this was not a matter she wished him to treat lightly.

"I suppose it wasn't too hard to guess," she said. "I would have told you when we were up at the house today, but I was afraid. I didn't know what you'd say to being saddled with a ready-made family."

"I was already saddled — your word, and not a nice one — with a ready-made family. All the signs are that Leo's getting dug in here, and the headmaster's report on the conditions in Joshua's hometown makes it unlikely that he'll be able to go there for some time, if ever. So I've got two of them. How do you feel about starting married life with two eight-year-old boys?"

"I think we can make them happy — them and the twins."

"But we have to house them. How much do you think those minor alterations you mentioned are going to cost?"

"Whatever they cost, wouldn't it be worth it? It's such a beautiful house."

"It could be. But what you meant by minor alterations was tearing the inside out and throwing it away and starting again. But to return to the twins, you want to adopt them?"

"I hadn't thought of adoption. I just know I want to keep them. Who else have they got but me? A mother who didn't want them and a father who doesn't seem to have any paternal feelings. I can't understand how a man like Julian, who's a good man, can be such a bad father. Or wouldn't you agree that he's a good man?"

"Good for what?"

"Good as opposed to bad. But not a good father."

"And at a guess, not much of a husband. He was miscast. The twins look enough like him to prove his paternity, but they must have taken his first and last ounce of virility. I'd say he's forgotten he was ever married. Once you've removed the twins, he'll forget he was ever a father. I've already got maiden aunts; he's going to make another. And now listen carefully to what I'm going to say. Adopt. It's a legal transaction, binding on all parties. If we take the twins, we take them over. We bring them up. They'll grow up thinking of us — you and me — as their natural parents. They'll be told who they are; your brother will see them whenever he wants to, he'll visit them and he might even remember to ask them to visit him. Apart from those privileges, he leaves them to us. He renounces his rights. If when they're grown up, they want to re-adopt him, fine; until then they're legally ours. You understand?"

"Yes."

"You agree?"

Agreeing, she noted that this was the first time she had ever heard him speak firmly, directly and without an undercurrent of provocation. It was her first glimpse of a side of him that she had

210

known existed, but had never seen.

"Do I tell him this?" she asked.

"We both tell him." He put out a hand and drew her down beside him. "Now that we've fixed our family, perhaps we can fix our wedding."

She sighed contentedly and settled into his arms. They did not speak for some time. Then she broke the silence.

"We've talked a lot about where we're going to live. Could I know what we're going to live on?"

"I've told you. At least, I've tried to tell you, in some form or other. Money's no problem."

"But your job?"

"I've been thinking it over. I don't feel that Downing's a place in which to try and sell or rent villas on the Continent. Downing's package-tour territory. They like to travel, but they like coming home at the end of the holiday. I don't think I could do any business here even if I sat in an office surrounded by posters displaying blue seas and golden beaches and bronzed nudes. I've got another job in mind, but it isn't a nine-to-five one. Would you feel insecure if you found yourself with a husband who doesn't do a daily dash to a director's desk?"

"No."

"I've never understood the biblical attitude to work. Adam was thrown out of that garden and told to apply to the nearest labour exchange. Sweat of his brow, I think the term was. Why was it uttered as a curse? We all know that if we're

211

doing work we like doing, we've reached the pinnacle of happiness. Isn't that true?"

"Mm."

"Are you listening?"

"Mm."

"What did I say last?"

"Congenial work is a blessing and not a curse."

"Underline congenial. I'm not talking about those poor chaps in the salt mines. Have we, for the moment, cleared up all our outstanding problems?"

"I think so. When are you going to tell the golf committee that you're not selling the house?"

"I've got until the end of the week. Anything else?"

"We've got to tell Julian about adopting the twins."

"We'll choose a moment when we can get his whole attention. At the moment it's given to orchestras. I suppose we'll also have to tell my aunts that we're getting married, but I'm not looking forward to their reactions. Squeals of joy, congratulations and then fuss, fuss, fuss. I like the way things are now — just you and me. Any more problems?"

"No."

"Do you love me?"

"Yes."

"Then let me show you another way of reaching the pinnacle of happiness."

Chapter

11

Miss Drew's departure had two immediate results. The first was a short, sharp note from Mrs. Gilling to Natalie, informing her that she was no longer disposed to search for domestic helpers. Miss Drew, she explained, had obtained the post at the school through her, and she had regarded her as a kind of protégée and was not prepared to overlook the way in which she had been treated by Mr. Travers.

Natalie wrote an even briefer note in reply, thanking Mrs. Gilling for her past kindness and regretting the unfortunate manner of Miss Drew's departure. She stamped the envelope, gave it to Mrs. Lingford to post and then proceeded to put into execution the second result of the incident.

It was sometimes better, she decided, to act first and explain afterwards. Accordingly she dressed the twins warmly, packed them into the car and set off for the town.

She drove to within a short distance of the shop called Hamil's and paused for a few minutes' reflection. She knew nothing about Mrs. Swayne. There had been no suggestion at the interview that she had ever looked after any children but her own. Her background was one of shadowy Indian figures. But there was a gap to be filled, and Natalie was here to ask her to fill it.

She drove on to a point at which she could see the twins from the shop, got out and entered.

Almost every shop in the town was by now dressed overall for the Christmas season. Cardboard bells swung from doorways; silver stars dangled from ceilings; the wares in the windows were arranged artistically round miniature figures of Father Christmas. The local paper had written a strong column pouring scorn on the shopkeepers in neighbouring towns who had made the steep rise in toy prices an excuse for discontinuing their annual presentation of Santa Claus in person. The leading Downing store had gone so far as to place a sled and two realistic reindeer at the entrance to its premises. But Mr. Hamil had confined his decorations to some wisps of cotton wool on the shelves and a few lengths of tinsel hanging wistfully in the window.

There were few customers in the shop. In the chicken-wire cage sat Mrs. Swayne, giving change to an Asian woman. At the back of the shop a small, wiry dark-skinned man was placing cans of beans along a shelf. Natalie guessed he was the owner. Ignoring him, she addressed Mrs. Swayne.

"Good morning. Is it possible for someone to take your place for a few minutes? I'd like to talk to you. I won't keep you long."

Mr. Hamil was at her elbow.

"You wish to talk?"

214

"To Mrs. Swayne, yes."

"She is busy, very busy. You can see. To leave is impossible, quite impossible."

"I see." She turned to Mrs. Swayne, her tone and manner giving no indication that they had ever met one another before. "My name is Travers — Miss Travers. Somebody told me that you might be free sometimes to undertake baby-sitting. The children are twins — you can see them outside in the car. If you could come when the shop is closed, someone would fetch you and take you back. The house is one of those that overlook the golf course."

"To baby-sit, this is what you have come to ask?" Mr. Hamil said in surprise.

"Yes." She gave him a brief glance before turning back to Mrs. Swayne. "This is my telephone number. I'll meet you anywhere you say, to arrange times and terms. But I hope you'll come. I'll leave dinner for you when I go out, or if you prefer, you can bring your own and charge me. Or you could cook it yourself — the twins would be in bed. You'll let me know?"

Mrs. Swayne, speechless, nodded. Then she threw a nervous glance at Mr. Hamil.

"If there's any difficulty" — Natalie spoke clearly, including the small, curious group of customers in the words — "please let me know. I'm sure we can clear it up. Are you free when the shop closes?"

"There is other things to do, you know," Mr. Hamil's tone had taken on a tinge of belliger-

215

ence. "A person cannot just shut the shop and go off in that way."

Natalie assumed a puzzled air.

"You mean that Mrs. Swayne works overtime?"

"I mean there are things to do, extra things."

"What time does she go home?"

"Home? This is her home, here. I am her brother-in-law, and I have given a home."

"Does she do overtime every evening?"

"Already I have told you. There is things to do."

Natalie addressed Mrs. Swayne.

"Thursday is early closing day, isn't it?"

Once again, Mrs. Swayne's only response was a timid nod.

"Then, unless I hear from you that it's impossible, could we say Thursday at six? Someone will call for you. Are you free on that evening?"

A third nod.

"Then until then . . ."

Natalie went back to the car. She had made a start; the rest was up to Mrs. Swayne. If she was to escape from the cage, even for short periods, she would have to deal with Mr. Hamil. If she couldn't, it might be possible to send in reinforcements.

She drove back to the house, humming a happy little air in which Randall joined. She thought that perhaps as well as making chairman's speeches like his uncle Maurice, he was going to be musical, like his father. Rowena gave no sign, so far, of being anything but beautiful.

216

At dinner that evening it became evident that it was not only Mrs. Swayne who would have to overcome opposition.

"I don't understand," Julian said irritably. "Which woman are you talking about?"

"The one who came after a job."

"But do you know anything about her?"

"Yes. She works in a shop that belongs to her brother-in-law."

"I meant did you, do you, know anything about her qualifications?"

"She's a widow. She —"

"Has she had any experience? Did you see her references? You can't leave the twins with anyone you haven't checked."

Even Henry, she found, was doubtful about introducing Mrs. Swayne to the baby-sitting post.

"All you're going on," he protested, "is what I suppose you'll claim is intuition."

"It isn't intuition at all. It's observation. I saw her; I spoke to her; I studied her, I liked her. I trust her."

"You feel sorry for her. You see her a victim of exploitation. How do you know that this Hamil isn't a decent shopkeeper who's been landed with a widowed sister-in-law who's appointed herself cashier and is stealing the contents of the till? She might even have staged that daylight robbery."

"I wish you'd stop being obstructive. You didn't see her. I did."

217

"And I will. I shall make a special visit to the shop, with or without you."

It was made with her. They drove to the shop, left the twins in the car and went inside.

Mrs. Swayne was not at the cash desk. Instead, the cage was occupied by a very stout Asian boy. Mr. Hamel, appearing from a room at the back of the shop, on being asked where Mrs. Swayne was, gave a smirk and shook his head.

"She is not here. She went away."

"Do you know where she went?" Henry inquired.

"London, perhaps. Perhaps not. Who knows? That is where she came from. She was not up to this work, so I gave her the sack."

"She's your sister-in-law, I understand. She must have left some address."

Mr. Hamil waggled his head.

"No. No address. I was not interested to find out this address, that address. She went of her own free accord. I washed my hands. You must look in London."

Natalie was about to speak, but Henry took her arm and led her out to the car.

"How," she asked hopelessly, as they drove away, "do you start looking for someone in London?"

"Why London?"

"He said so."

"He was lying."

"She did at least have a job and a kind of

home. I've ruined it all. She's gone."

"My guess is that she hasn't gone far. Why would she go back to London? If she has any sense at all, she'll know that she can do better in a place like this than in a wilderness like London. If she'd had any friends there, she wouldn't have come to Downing. You'll find she hasn't gone far."

"Then why hasn't she been in touch with me?"

"Probably because she didn't want you to feel responsible for what happened — which indicates a certain consideration. When she came to see you, surely she gave you some kind of lead, some address at which you could get hold of her?"

"No. Only the shop. She didn't . . . Yes, she did! She did! I remember now. Please turn and go back. She said I could go to the baker's shop on the corner."

Henry drove to the baker's. Here it was merely a matter of question and answer.

"Can you tell me where Mrs. Swayne is?"

"Mrs. Swayne? Back of the shop, love. This way."

A section of the counter was lifted. They went through a door at the end of the shop and found themselves in a neat sitting room. The door to the kitchen was open; they saw Mrs. Swayne standing before a stove, stirring the contents of a frying pan. There was a strong smell of curry.

She turned and saw them. She stood motionless for a moment and then put down the wooden spoon, lowered the gas and joined them.

"Miss Travers, you went to the shop again?"

"Yes. He said you'd gone to London. Why didn't you get in touch with me?"

"I wanted to. But what could I say to you? That I am sacked from Mr. Hamil's shop? You would think that it was because you came and spoke to me that day. So I came here. I am the cook and I have a room and I am on trial for two weeks, and if I am all right, they will keep me on. So I was going to say to you: My job is changed, but I would like to come whenever you want me to, to look after the babies."

"Shall we say next Friday?"

"Yes. Thank you."

"Somebody'll call for you and bring you back."

Mrs. Swayne looked from her to Henry and gave him a slow smile.

"You are the brother?" she asked him.

"No. The future husband."

"You are a very lucky gentleman. You know?"

"Not yet. I hope to find out."

He went to fetch her on Friday afternoon. He and Natalie did not go out; they spent the afternoon watching the twins getting acquainted with the new baby-sitter. Mrs. Swayne had brought with her some small picture books with rather lurid Indian illustrations; seated on the carpet with an attentive twin on either side of her, she told them why the youth was dancing and the maiden was weeping. She handled the children with an ease and expertise that were impressive, and they were not pleased when she left them and drove away with Henry.

With a reliable baby-sitter to depend on, Natalie decided that she could now accept dinner invitations. There had been several of these which she had felt no regret at refusing, since they had come from unattached masters at the school. But there had been some parties she would have liked to go to.

But before going to any parties, she wanted to give one. She put her idea before Henry.

"Do you think your aunt Blanche and her husband would come to dinner one evening?"

"Out to dinner with us?"

"No. Dinner at Julian's house. Couldn't I invite them in an informal, next-door-neighbour way?"

"She'd come, but I don't think he would. She says the doctor's told him to take it easy. When did you think of asking them?"

"On Wednesday week. I'd like eight people: the headmaster and his wife, your aunt and her husband, Julian and myself and two more."

"One of which would be me. Thank you for your kind invitation."

Julian was less pleased at the idea.

"You mean *here?*" he asked in surprise.

"Yes."

"Be an awful sweat. And expensive. All those drinks."

"You can afford it."

"Well, as long as you limit it to three or four. You can't hold receptions in a house this size."

"You and me. Mr. and Mrs. Wray. The headmaster and his wife."

"That'll make the half dozen. We can manage those."

"I'd like to ask that newly married couple, the science master and his wife. She's rather nice. We met at the hairdresser's. And Henry Downing and one of the school secretaries, to make a pair."

"That's too many. What do you want to ask Downing for?"

"I just told you. To make a pair with the school secretary."

"Not at all necessary. And why the married couple? She'll want to sing. Somebody told me she's got a voice and likes showing off."

"That's not this wife. That's the geography master's wife, and she doesn't sing. She does monologues."

"I don't see why we should rush into entertaining a lot of people. It isn't as though you're going to settle down here."

"Call it the Christmas spirit. We'll be ten. Eight thirty on Wednesday week, if they can come."

"I would have thought you had enough to do without embarking on a cooking session for all those people."

"I'm not embarking, I'm experimenting. I'm going to ask Mrs. Swayne to do the dinner."

"Mrs. Swayne? What on —"

"She doesn't only baby-sit. She's a cook."

"Have you ever eaten anything she's cooked?"

"No."

"Then how do you know what sort of messes she'll produce? You might find yourself landed with the kind of food they serve on motorways."

"Don't worry; we'll all eat well."

"When do you plan to have this affair?"

"I just told you — Wednesday week. It depends on how much notice the headmaster and his wife need."

They did not need more than a week. But the numbers were reduced by two: Mrs. Wray accepted for herself but said it would not be possible for her husband to go out, even so short a distance, at night. Natalie therefore paired her with Henry and added only the science master and his bride.

Having issued the invitations, Natalie informed Mrs. Lingford that the dining room was to be used. Mrs. Lingford gave no sign of having heard, but by degrees the room was cleared of its extraneous objects. The sewing machine went upstairs. The children's toys were put into a cupboard. The sideboard was pushed below the hatch that opened to the kitchen, and the chairs were ranged in orderly fashion round the table.

But Mrs. Swayne, asked to undertake the dinner, showed signs of panic.

"Oh, Miss Travers," she moaned, "you don't know what you are asking! My cooking is not your sort, not your sort at all. It is Indian, you know? The people I am working for, the bakers, they like everything hot, so hot that they will take roasted chillies. I didn't think that English people would be able to eat things like that. But for your friends, I don't think . . ."

"I thought we could talk over some simple menus and choose one of them. What I'd like to do is leave it all to you and just ask you not to burn everybody's tongues off."

Mrs. Swayne's countenance began to clear.

"What I will do," she said, "is make you some little bits of some dishes and ask the baker to bring them here. Then you can say which is best. But perhaps the guests you are asking will not like Indian cooking. So many people think that this is only mulligatawny soup and curry, but that is nonsense."

"No soup. We'll start with fish."

"I will make you myhee molee. And after that —"

"You'll probably want ingredients that I haven't got. Spices and things."

"My brother-in-law, Mr. Hamil, has everything for Indian cooking. It was through me that he began to sell them, and now a lot of people go and buy."

"Do you still see him?"

"I go and talk sometimes. I don't like to quarrel with anybody. But I won't go and see his mother. No, never. For the end of your dinner, Miss Travers, what would you like me to give?"

"That's easy. Indian sweets, please. I know you're making them now and selling them at the baker's, and so many of the schoolchildren are buying them that it would be nice to demonstrate to the headmaster how good and wholesome they are. Will you get everything you need and add it to my bill?"

The night of the party was cold, but fine. Julian had been prodded into buying and putting out drinks. He refused to offer his best brandy; Miss Drew's boyfriend, he said bitterly, had sufficiently lowered the level in the bottle.

Henry arrived early, too early to go next door and fetch Mrs. Wray. Natalie ordered him out of the kitchen and sent him to talk to Julian in the drawing room.

When Mrs. Wray arrived, she expressed her husband's disappointment at not being present.

"But he couldn't have come," she said. "He won't admit it, but I know he isn't feeling well."

Natalie said that she was sorry and settled her in a chair with a drink.

The headmaster and his wife arrived next. Last and late arrivals were the science master and his wife. The bride was wearing a maternity dress which, frilled and flounced and designed to conceal her advanced stage of pregnancy, served only to accentuate it. Her husband led her to a chair and tenderly surrounded her with cushions.

"Comfortable, darling?" he inquired.

"Go away. You've done enough damage," she snapped. "He *fusses,*" she told the assembled guests in exasperated tones. "You'd think I'd volunteered for one of those experimental diseases. It isn't a disease, and I didn't volunteer. Oh, Natalie, when am I going to look lovely like you again?"

"You look lovely as you are," Natalie told her with sincerity. "Can you eat and drink everything we give you?"

"I eat like a horse, and I drink like a fish. The shape I am, other pleasures are diminishing."

The headmaster, watching her from across the room, wore a slight look of speculation. This was rather an exotic bird to introduce into a conservative cage.

"We're having an Indian meal," Natalie announced. "Cooked not by me, but by an expert."

"Curry? Aphrodisiac," the bride said. "I'm warning you."

"Not curry."

Natalie took a bowl of olives to Mrs. Wray, who had lost the look of worry she had worn on her arrival.

"I don't think," she remarked, "that Henry has spent so much time in Downing since his schooldays."

"All he's done," said the headmaster, "is drop in from time to time to let us know he's not staying. I still hope he'll be seized one day with a desire to put down roots here. But he won't."

"Yes, he will," Henry said. "I can feel them growing."

"He'd be an unpopular citizen," Julian said.

"Ever since the news got round that he isn't selling Downing House, people have —"

"I know. Taken against him, as the saying is. In my opinion," the headmaster said, "it's time he did something for the town."

"You're going to abuse the Downings," said Mrs. Wray. "I feel it coming."

"Abuse? No. Reproach, yes. You can't deny, Blanche, that for three hundred years and more your family has failed to live up to its obligations. The Downings were at one time the only family of substance in the district. They had land; they sold it and got money. The town began to grow, and went on growing, and they sat back and watched it spreading, haphazard, without any kind of plan."

"Town planning came much later," Mrs. Wray pointed out.

"Don't try to change the subject. The trouble has always been," the headmaster went on, "that Downing didn't start as a hamlet or a village. It never had any tradition. It sprang up from the sites that incoming traders bought from the Downings. It began with small trade and went on to bigger trade. Shops, offices, workshops — all began to merge into a town, but a town without a central point, with no pivot, no family to give them a lead. So it lacked, and still lacks, amenities, institutions that a leading family would have provided, or seen were provided."

"As, for example?" asked the science master.

"There's no organized help for the old or the

sick in their own homes. There's a park with swings, but no adequate children's playground. There's no nursery. I've done what I could in the forty or so years I've been here, but what was needed was the weight of those three hundred years. The maternity wing of the hospital is thirty years out of date."

"Fifty," corrected the bride. "The minute I got pregnant, I went and took a look. I'm going to have my baby in the science lab. And while you're listing omissions, write down that there aren't more than two decent pubs, either ancient with inglenooks or modern with jukeboxes."

"When they built an arts center," Mrs. Wray reminded them, "they had to close it down. That wasn't the Downings' fault, was it?"

"Yes, it was. No lead from the top. No patrons. No imaginative program," the headmaster said.

"Aren't you being a bit overambitious?" his wife asked. "After all, Downing's rather a rural wilderness, dozing while the world passes it by."

"Oh, no, it isn't," the bride answered. "I've been researching. This town can claim to be in the main stream of world events. This year alone, five robberies with assault, fourteen muggings, eighty-two driving-under-the-influence, one bank holdup and an unspecified number of strikes. What's more, the local beauty queen came fifteenth in the Miss England competition, and a Downing butcher stood for Parliament and nearly got in. And another statistic coming: A

Downing bull was almost sold to a buyer in Argentina."

There was silence as the guests took in these figures.

"We used to pray for peace in our time, O Lord," Mrs. Whitestone reminisced.

"I always thought that was a selfish prayer," said Mrs. Wray. "Why not peace at all times, O Lord?"

"There you go again — changing the subject," complained the headmaster. "I'm trying to direct Henry's attention to his duty towards the town."

"What would you like me to make a start on?" Henry asked. "You may not believe it, but I've been giving a lot of thought to the subject recently. I agree that after three hundred years of sitting back and doing nothing, it's time I bestirred myself. I already have, in one direction."

"And — which direction is that?" the headmaster asked.

"Well, it's only a modest beginning. I've decided to give the golfers a clubhouse."

"*Give?*" Julian asked.

"That's right; give."

"Downing House?"

"No. Not Downing House. I have other plans for Downing House. What I'm proposing to do is build a clubhouse on the foundations of the lodge that Sinjon Downing never got round to finishing."

"Build a clubhouse?" Julian peered at him, adjusted his glasses and left them at a rakish angle. "*Build* one? Are you serious?"

"Would I presume to make jokes in the presence of my old headmaster?"

"When did you think of this scheme?" the headmaster asked.

"Some time ago. Several minutes, in fact. I'm going to build a clubhouse, and anyone who has any ideas about what it should contain in the way of accommodation can come and see me — at the hotel. By appointment."

"It's a start," conceded the headmaster. "But it only takes care of the golfers."

"Get to work on the new maternity wing," urged the bride. "I shan't be needing it myself in the next ten years, but do you know how many pregnant women there are at this moment in — this town?"

"No. How should I know?" Henry asked.

"There are one hundred and forty-seven, in various stages of anticipation. Incidentally, are you related to those two old Edwardian ducks who inhabit one of the hotel cottages?"

"My sisters," said Mrs. Wray.

"My aunts. But they're not Edwardian; they're Georgian. Did they promise you a Christmas hamper?"

"Yes."

"They promised it to me, too. And to Natalie. We'll all go shares."

A timid signal on Julian's Swiss cowbell, placed in the kitchen for Mrs. Swayne, told

Natalie that dinner was ready. She led the guests into the dinning room. Mrs. Wray, the first to enter, paused on the threshold.

"Natalie, how lovely!"

Natalie, on the point of agreeing, gave a modest smile instead. She had transformed a somewhat dull room and given it charm. The table gleamed with the silver which she was to have inherited but which had been given instead to Julian. A low bowl of flowers flanked by candles stood in the center of the table. It was not quite up to Freddie's standards, she thought, but it would do.

She had wasted no time worrying about what the meal would be like. She had helped with a few preliminaries in the kitchen and had been reassured. For although Mrs. Swayne, wearing long, dangling earrings and several brooches, had not presented the orthodox picture of a cook, there had been an impressive professionalism about the way she rolled up her sleeves, donned a large apron and set to work.

The fish was handed in through the hatch, smelling delicious and delicately flavoured with coconut. With the unusual meat dish that followed, there was unanimous agreement that the cook was an artist. Mrs. Swayne, drawing back the sliding door of the hatch and appearing briefly to hand in or take away dishes and plates, was greeted finally by a chorus of congratulation.

Nobody left early except Mrs. Wray. Henry

took her to her gate and returned to find that Joshua had become the subject of the conversation.

"He's got a happy disposition," the headmaster was saying. "He'll need it later on. At the moment, all he's thinking about is Christmas. He's doing a song-and-dance act at the end-of-term concert. I thought it was a good idea until I looked in at rehearsal."

"I looked in, too," said the science master. "Pure savage. No music, as we know it; no words you could call words. A few yells and what I suppose is a junior war dance — but I found it eerie. A kind of jungle interlude."

Natalie sat listening contentedly; the party had been a success. When at last all the guests but Henry had departed, she went into the kitchen to thank Mrs. Swayne and to help with the last of the clearing-up. Left with Henry, Julian spoke anxiously.

"Look, I'm not quite clear what you mean about the clubhouse. You build it and we buy it?"

"I build it and I donate it. It's rather a selfish way of doing it — I want the fun of planning. But I'm open to suggestions."

"You've made up your mind? I mean, this is really on?"

"It's definite, yes."

"Then I've got a few ideas, if you'd care to hear them sometime."

"Anytime."

Julian opened the cupboard.

"I think we ought to drink to it, don't you?"

"Good idea."

Natalie, emerging from the kitchen with Mrs. Swayne, watched with surprise the last of the brandy disappearing. With even more surprise, she heard Julian, when Henry and Mrs. Swayne had driven away, express the opinion that the evening had been a great success.

"Though I don't mind admitting," he went on, "that when I saw that woman in the kitchen, I had my doubts. I was afraid we were going to find a couple of earrings in the food. But it was a good meal. You take the most unjustified risks at times, but you usually seem to pull it off. What do you think of this proposition of Downing's?"

"To build a clubhouse?"

"Yes. I'll feel better when he's met the golf committee and put something down in writing."

Getting ready for bed, Natalie looked back with satisfaction on the evening. It might, she thought, be the beginning of a new career for Mrs. Swayne; both Mrs. Whitestone and the science master's wife had gone away determined to ask her to cook for their future parties.

She glanced out of her window before getting into bed. Stars, and a very cold night. Only a dim light in the hall next door, but it was enough to show Mr. Wray's bedroom still empty, still with his dressing gown hanging on the rail of the bed. She pictured him in his wife's room, listening to details of the party he had missed.

She woke to find that it was dark — not the morning darkness of winter, but a predawn darkness. Something had wakened her — she thought of the twins, got up and put on a dressing gown and went across the landing to look at them. Both were fast asleep. From Julian's room came the sound of gentle or gentlemanly snores. She went back to her room and switched off the light and was about to go back to bed when she realized that a light was on in the house next door. She went to the window and looked out. Mr. Wray's bedroom was brightly illuminated. Mrs. Wray was rolling up his dressing gown and putting it into an opened suitcase. She went to a drawer, took out some clothing and put it into the case. Then she closed the case, lifted it off the bed and carried it to the door and switched off the light. A moment later the light above the front door came on. Natalie, increasingly uneasy, saw her walking down the flagged path holding not one suitcase, but two. She reached her car, put one case into the back and the other on the seat beside the driver's; then she got in, started the car and drove away.

Natalie, unable to guess what had happened, was left with a guilty feeling of having done nothing to help. She should, she thought, have opened the window and called to Mrs. Wray as she was going out to the car; she should have asked whether where was anything she could do. Where was Mr. Wray? Had he been taken ill during the night? Had his wife telephoned for an ambulance, and was she now following it, with his luggage and her own?

There was nothing to be learned by staring out the window. The outside light was still switched on next door; perhaps that meant that Mrs. Wray would soon be returning.

It was almost six o'clock. She went back to bed and lay dozing until seven.

She asked Julian at breakfast if he had heard any sounds during the night from next door.

"No. Were there sounds?"

"I saw Mrs. Wray driving away just before six. I think he must have been taken ill."

Julian was not unduly interested. He was scraping the bottom of the marmalade jar.

"Can't you make some homemade marmalade?" he asked. "I don't like this bought stuff. I wish you'd make some of that mixed lemon and grapefruit you used to make in Brighton."

"I will if you like."

The telephone rang. Julian, nearest to it, reached out and picked up the receiver.

"For you. Mrs. Wray," he told Natalie.

She took the receiver from him and heard Mrs. Wray's voice.

"I'm speaking from London, Natalie. I'm afraid I've bad news. I had to drive Marcus up here early this morning. He's in hospital. I'll let you have more news later, but what I'm ringing for now is to ask you please to tell Henry that I left a light on outside the house. I may have left some on inside, too. He knows where the keys are."

"I'll tell him. I'm so sorry to hear —"

She stopped; the line was dead. She handed the receiver back to Julian, and he replaced it.

"She's in London," she told him. "Her husband's in hospital. I wish I'd asked her this morning if there was anything I could do to help."

Julian was putting on his coat in the hall.

"I never thought of asking how old he was," he said. "Did you ever find out?"

"No. Somewhere in his sixties, I suppose."

"Well, let's hope he survives. She looked as though she was enjoying married life. 'Bye."

He opened the front door and gave an exclamation of annoyance.

"What is it?" Natalie asked.

"Snow. Dammit, it's too early for snow."

Too early or not, at the end of an hour there was a covering of snow on the branches of the trees, and the lane was white and slippery. Henry, appearing at half past ten, had snowflakes on his coat.

"It's not going to last." He stood on the steps and looked at the sky. "It's going to turn to rain."

"Come inside."

"No. Put on your coat and come out. We're going next door —"

"Your aunt rang."

"I know. She told me. Can you leave the twins for a while?"

"Yes. They're all right, and Mrs. Lingford will

236

call me if they're not."

She threw a coat around her shoulders, called to Mrs. Lingford to tell her she was going next door and walked beside Henry, head down against the sleety downpour. He stopped at Mrs. Wray's door, tilted the tub of fern beside it and stooped to pick up a latchkey.

"What time did she ring you?" Natalie asked.

"About half an hour ago."

"How is he?"

He ushered her into the hall.

"He's dead," he answered.

The overcoat she was about to hang up fell from her hands. She turned slowly to face him.

"Did you say . . ."

"Dead." He switched off the outside light. "She asked me to come in here and clear up."

"Clear up what?"

"All his things. She doesn't want to come back to them." They were in the bedroom into which Natalie had so often glanced. Henry took a large suitcase from a cupboard, placed it on the floor, opened it and then began to go through the drawers, taking out piles of neatly folded clothing.

"Will you start on the stuff in the wardrobe?" he asked.

She began mechanically to remove suits from their hangers.

"What happened?" she asked.

"She called me from London and told me what had happened. He'd got worse during the night, and they decided he'd have to go to hospital. She packed two suitcases — his and hers — and put them in the car and then got him into his dressing gown and slippers and helped him down the path and into the car. Then she drove nonstop to London. She . . . What's the matter?"

She shook her head to clear it.

"Nothing. I mean . . . Didn't he go in an ambulance?"

"No. She drove him."

"But —"

"But what?"

"Nothing."

Folding suits, packing them, she tried to get her thoughts into order. This room . . . she had never seen him in it. That desk . . . she had never seen him seated at it.

She went over and opened the drawers. All were empty.

His dressing gown. It had hung on this rail, and Mrs. Wray had rolled it up and put it into a suitcase. He had not had it on. And he had not been in the car.

Henry was leaning against the wardrobe, watching her.

"Something worrying you?" he asked.

She stared at him and then walked slowly to the bed and took a firm grasp of the rail. She spoke unsteadily.

"But you . . . you saw him! You *saw* him! Don't you remember what you said? You said he looked . . . he looked scholarly. Don't you remember?"

"Yes, I remember." He sat on the bed and pulled her down beside him. "I also said that he looked frail."

"You saw him. You said so."

"Somebody had to see him. He was growing into a mystery man, and Clarice and Geraldine would soon have become suspicious. I don't think they would ever have guessed, but other people might have. So somebody had to see him. I said he looked scholarly, but when I'd thought it over, I decided that he ought to look frail, too. I told the Whitestones, hoping it would get round to Blanche. It did, and that gave her her cue. After that, it was easy for her; all she had to do was polish him off before any more parties could take place."

There was silence. After a time Natalie spoke in bewilderment.

"I don't understand. A different kind of person, a different kind of woman might have planned it, carried it out. But . . . but not her. I can't believe it."

"She had years to think about it, remember. She must have realized a long time ago that marriage was her only way of shaking off her sisters. But by the time my grandfather died her chances of marriage had died, too. So she had to invent a husband. The cruise took care of the beginning. His weak constitution took care of the end."

"When did you know?"

"Almost from the start. She made a few mistakes, one of them being to order all his suits from my grandfather's tailor. Same mode, same make. They sent the bill to Downing House, and I opened it by mistake, but I didn't let her know that I had. I didn't think it would be long before you began to make guesses. You could see that desk from your window; you could see his bed."

Silence fell once more. She sat in thought, and he waited.

"Why didn't you tell me?" she asked at last.

"Several reasons. First, I knew the thing couldn't go on for long. Second, I knew that you could see into this room and would soon realize that he was never in it and had never been in it. Third and last, you'd met two of my aunts; you might have written them off as merely eccentric, but I wanted their effect to wear off before telling you that I had a third aunt who invented husbands."

"But when she heard that you'd seen him, she must have realized that you —"

"— suspected something? No. She would have decided that I'd seen someone I thought could have been her husband."

She looked round the neat, bright room.

"She'll be lonely in this house all by herself."

"No, she won't. She'll be very happy. She's used to being on her own, and she's got a lot to keep her occupied. She's a good gardener, and she's a good needlewoman. She'll give small parties for her friends, and she'll cherish the Siamese kitten that you and I are going to present her with. She'll make a very contented widow."

"Where is he . . . What about the funeral?"

"Very quiet, very private, she told me. Cremation, ashes over his favourite walk in some unspecified woods. Have we got all this stuff in?"

"Yes. What are you going to do with it?"

"Take it to the headmaster's wife, who'll sell it and give the money to charity. You're still looking worried. Why? Do you feel she had a kind of crazy streak that I might have inherited?"

"I could have understood that better — craziness. But this planning . . . I can't believe she could have gone through with it."

"She was under strong pressure. She had to get away from Clarice and Geraldine. So she found herself a husband, and he's no more. *Requiescat in pace.* Come to think of it, she's the one who's going to rest in peace. And speaking of rest, this bed was mine once. I was promoted to it from a cot, but they found that I got out of it and took nocturnal walks round the house, so I was put back into the cot. I offered the bed to Blanche when she married, but I didn't realize it was so comfortable. I think I'll ask for it back. They're good springs, aren't they?"

"Yes."

"How do you know unless you lie back and test them? That's better. Are you still feeling sad? Are you grieving for Marcus Wray?"

"No. Are you sure she won't know you knew?"

"Quite sure. Are you comfortable?"

"Yes. But how can she sign her name as Wray when she never was?"

"That's her problem. I wish ceilings were more interesting. We should be gazing up at cherubim and seraphim. Perhaps they used to paint all those little Cupids on ceilings so that people in bed and in love would feel they were in good company. Did you know that some of his arrows engendered love but others had quite the opposite effect? Why aren't more girls named Aphrodite?"

"I don't know. When she comes back, will we have to pretend we're sorry she's been widowed?"

"You're not going to let this thing prey on your mind, are you?"

"No."

"Good. Are you —"

"You just asked me."

"Asked you what?"

"If I was comfortable. I said yes."

Chapter

12

Much sympathy was felt for Mrs. Wray when the news of her loss became known. To wait for so long before finding a husband, only to have him for so short a time, seemed to everyone a misfortune indeed. Henry and Natalie, going daily to her house, found letters of condolence filling the wire cage affixed to the inside of the front door and piled them on the hall table to await Mrs. Wray's return. She was in Italy; she had written to Henry to tell him that she was staying for a time with Leo's mother. She gave no further details about her husband's illness; her letter ended with a request to keep her house aired and her indoor plants watered.

"This letter" — Henry took one from the pile and held it up — "is from Geraldine."

"Calling for a truce, do you think?" Natalie asked.

"No. It'll be three lines of formal so-sorry-to-hear. They'll never get together again — they're too happy as they are. If I fetch and carry Mrs. Swayne to twin-sit, will you come out to dinner with me tonight?"

"Yes. Thank you."

He brought her home after dinner and took Mrs. Swayne away. Julian had shut himself into

243

his study to work, and she did not disturb him. But as she was going upstairs to bed, the telephone rang, and she came down again to answer it. It was Henry's voice. "I've just got back to the hotel. I've news for you. Your brother's here."

"But he —"

"Not Julian. The other one. Maurice."

"Maurice — here?"

"And Freddie."

"Freddie and Maurice?" she exclaimed in horror.

"I knew you'd be pleased."

"Where are they?"

"They checked into the hotel for the night. I saw them quite by chance — they didn't see me. They went up to their room, came down again and went out. I think I know where they've gone."

"How long ago?"

"About five minutes."

"Henry, please come."

"*Me?*"

"Please."

"Don't be silly. This is purely a family occasion."

"I know why they've come."

"So do I. To find out what's keeping you."

"*Please* come."

"If I come, I shall tell them I'm joining the family."

"Tell them anything you like, but *come.*"

She rang off and opened the study door.

"Julian, Maurice and Freddie are on their way here. *Julian.*"

He looked up, his expression first vague and then irritated.

"What is it?"

"Maurice and Freddie."

"I do wish you wouldn't interrupt when I'm —"

"Maurice and Freddie are coming."

"Who?"

"Will you *listen?* Maurice and Freddie. They're on their way."

"On their way where?"

"Here."

"Here?"

"Yes. They'll be here within minutes, unless they lose their way."

"Did you say they were actually on their way here?"

"Yes. Will you stop whatever it is you're doing and come out and meet them?"

"How do you know they're coming?"

"What does it matter how I know? The point is that they're coming, and they haven't come to be friendly."

"It must be about domestic help. Wasn't Freddie trying the London agencies? Perhaps she's found someone."

"She wouldn't come all this way to tell us that. She'd ring."

He pushed back his chair and rose. He had a hunted air.

"Can't we slip away and dodge them?" he asked. "Let's go out the back way and —"

"Your car's outside, and so is mine. And here they are."

Even the summons, she thought, going to answer it, sounded like a call to arms. She opened the door, and Maurice and Freddie entered. Over their shoulders she saw, with infinite thankfulness, Henry's car turning in at the gate. Maurice paused and gave it a look of displeasure.

"Surely not visitors at this hour?" he said.

Julian was at the door of the drawing room. Natalie passed Maurice and Freddie over to him and turned to wait for Henry.

When everybody was assembled in the drawing room, Maurice glanced at Henry and then spoke.

"We've been visiting friends. Freddie suggested a detour on the way home, to look in here. We wanted to have a talk, a family talk, but . . ."

"You're going to say that it's purely a family matter," Henry said. "That's why I'm here, too. I don't think you and your wife remember me, but we met in London. Twice. The last time was at the Spanish Embassy."

"I remember now," Freddie said. "What are you doing in this town?"

"I live here. It's rather a coincidence that you should turn up tonight. What I came to say can be said to you both as well as to Julian. It was about my marrying Natalie."

Silence fell. All eyes were on him. Julian looked bewildered, Freddie looked angry and Maurice looked suspicious. Natalie had the air

246

of a spectator unaffected by the proceedings.

"You'd better explain," Maurice said coldly. "My sister is, as I understand it, on the point of becoming engaged."

"That's what I'm saying. We decided to tell Julian — and there was also another matter we had to discuss with him. Since we're all here, we can talk it over, and it'll save relaying it to you later."

"This is the first I've heard of any —" Julian began.

Freddie addressed Natalie.

"Rather sudden, isn't it?" she asked. "Or did you know each other before you came here?"

"No. We didn't."

"I suppose you haven't forgotten that Michael Morley's on his way home?"

"In the full expectation," Maurice added, "of finding you waiting for him."

"Then he hasn't been reading my letters," Natalie said. "They were clear enough. I told him before he left England, and I've confirmed it twice in writing since, that I hadn't and haven't any intention of marrying him."

They were too angry for speech, and she found herself feeling sorry for them. The Morley family connections would have given luster to Freddie's receptions; his political pull would have been very useful indeed to Maurice. It must be bitter to see him superseded by a stranger whose sole credential seemed to be an appearance at the Spanish Embassy.

"I suppose you know what you're doing?"

247

Freddie asked at last.

"Yes."

"I told you you were going to be trapped when you came here, but I didn't dream of anything like this."

"I don't like it," Maurice said. "I think you've lost your head."

"No, she didn't do that," Henry reassured him. "She didn't get carried off her feet either. We thought it over very carefully."

"Perhaps we can be informed when you plan to get married."

"As soon as Natalie decides on a date. There's nothing to hold us up."

"No?" inquired Freddie. "Perhaps, as Julian seems to have forgotten them, I might ask who is going to take over the two children."

"The twins?" Henry turned to Julian. "This seems as good a time as any other to tell you what Natalie and I have been discussing. We want to adopt them."

"Adopt them?" Julian repeated the words in a tone between astonishment and bewilderment. "*Adopt* them?"

"Yes, adopt them," Natalie confirmed. "We want to take them over and bring them up. They'll see you often, I hope, but I also hope they'll grow up looking on Henry and me as their natural parents. Apart from visits, you must leave them to us."

"What she means," said Henry, "is that you renounce your claim on them."

Julian stared at him and then transferred his gaze to Natalie.

"Bit sudden, isn't it?" he asked.

"It's not at all sudden," she answered. "Ever since I came here, it's been obvious that I wasn't going to hand them over to a stranger. Freddie was right when she said I'd be trapped, but she was wrong about the kind of trap. If you married again, and your wife wanted the twins, there might have to be a rethink, but I don't think you'll marry again, and I want the twins, and so does Henry."

"I see." He paused. "I'll miss them."

"I think you will — every now and then. But they won't be far away."

Julian addressed Henry.

"You said, a little while ago, that you lived here. But you don't."

"From now on I do."

"Live here?"

"Yes."

"Here in Downing, permanently?"

"Yes. In the house you once thought might be turned into a clubhouse."

"You're going to live in Downing House?"

"After having some minor alterations done, yes."

"That doesn't mean, does it" — a note of sharp anxiety sounded in Julian's tone — "that you're going back on the idea of building a clubhouse?"

"No."

"Look here," Maurice said. "We came here —"

Julian, without glancing in his direction, waved him to silence.

"In that case," he told Henry, "I'd like to put some suggestions before you. You did say you were willing to consider suggestions, didn't you?"

"I did."

"What I was thinking was that there ought to be changing rooms and —"

"If you'll kindly —" Maurice began once more.

"— two or three sets of rooms for bachelors. We get a lot of good golfers, well-known ones, coming here for competitions, and they don't all care to stay in the hotel. The sets of rooms could be used intermittently, or permanently if a fellow wanted to live in them. What d'you think?"

"A very good idea."

"Will you kindly postpone this discussion to some other time," Maurice requested furiously, "and pay some attention to —"

"Oh, give up, for God's sake," Freddie said in a voice choked with rage. "Let's get out."

Maurice walked to the door and opened it.

"We've done our best," he informed Natalie. "From now on you can do as you like. Freddie and I won't go to any more trouble for nothing, I can assure you. Good-bye. We'll see ourselves out."

The front door banged behind them with a force that made the pram rattle. Julian spoke anxiously.

"You don't think they'll come back, do you?"

"No, I don't," Natalie answered.

"They might decide to come round in the morning."

"They won't."

"I hope you're right. Come to think of it, their sole object was to get you married to that chap Morley, and as that's fallen through, they'll probably leave us alone." He took off his glasses, studied them absently and put them on again. "Though I do rather agree with what they said about the short time you two have known each other."

"Long enough," Henry said.

"I hope it works out better than my marriage did. What happens about your work? You had an agency of some kind in Italy, I understood."

"I had. I'm giving it up."

"To do what?"

"I've decided to go in for farming."

"I see. Well, I wish you both luck. You won't mind if I turn in? It's been a rather upsetting evening."

"Not at all. Good night."

"Pity I didn't get in some more of that good brandy, to celebrate." He turned at the door. "Bit of a gamble, marriage."

"So they say."

"Well, good night. Good night, Natalie."

The door closed.

"Brotherly blessing, brotherly advice," Natalie commented. "Now will you please go home and let me lock up?"

"Presently. I'll wait until I've got your ruffled feathers smoothed down."

When she was seated with his arms round her, she spoke dreamily.

"Where's your farm?"

"The Crouches are giving up. I'm taking over."

"Do you know anything about farming?"

"No. Do you?"

"No."

"It's not complicated. You just have to rotate the crops and switch on the milking machines."

"I don't have to. You have to. We've got some odd relations, haven't we?"

"Mine are odder than yours. Are you prepared to cope with Clarice and Geraldine?"

"I'll stand by and watch you coping."

"They're issuing tickets for another concert."

"Louis du Boulay again?"

"No. An opera singer."

"Room booked at the hotel?"

"Provisionally, yes. Someone might surprise them by turning up one day. Are you feeling less ruffled?"

"I'm feeling sleepy. You can go home now."

"Soon. To return for a moment to Belmont, do you remember what you said to Bassanio when he got through that interminable speech and at last opened the casket?"

"Yes. I said, 'This house, these servants and this same myself are yours, my lord.' "

"Would you have handed them over?"

"The house and the servants? No."

"I'm sorry to hear it. That means you're not going to give me your Brighton property."

"Of course I'm not. Were you counting on it?"

"Certainly I was. You don't believe, do you, that marriage is the gamble your brother said it was?"

"No."

"Would you like me to read your future?"

She put out a hand, palm upward, and he took it and peered at the lines.

"You're going on a voyage."

"Is that all?"

"No. You've got to watch out for a dark man, rather good-looking, aged about thirty-three."

"I will. Next?"

"Children. I can see several. Animals, too."

"Of course. Dogs, cats, guinea pigs, hamsters, rabbits —"

"No. Bigger than those. Cows. You're going to marry a farmer. But you're not going to live on the farm. You're going to live in a nice big house with lovely gardens round it. Not at once. It isn't ready yet — there's a sort of break in this line. I can see a house much smaller . . . strange, it looks exactly like this one. You're going to stay in it while you're waiting for the big house to be ready. There was someone in this house, but . . . yes, he's gone."

"Where to?"

"His house wasn't ready either, so he went to

live next door to two old ladies in one of the hotel cottages until his bachelor quarters in the new clubhouse are ready. Then you go away from this house and go to live in your nice big one, and two more people come to this house. A man and a woman. The man looks to me like a kind of retired headmaster. He . . . don't take your hand away. I haven't finished."

She was looking at him with wide eyes.

"No, you've got it wrong," she said. "Not a man and a woman. Two men and two women."

"No. Only two people."

"Four people. Four and a half."

"Four and a half?"

"Of course. You don't suppose she'd let them go anywhere else, do you?"

"Who wouldn't let who go anywhere else?"

"The headmaster's wife wouldn't let the Days go to anyone else. She'd be crazy if she didn't keep them. She said herself that they were wonderful workers. She — ?"

He held up a hand to check her.

"Haven't you done enough juggling in this town?" he asked.

"Juggling?"

"You robbed the school of a good matron. You robbed a shop of a competent cashier. Now you're proposing to foist a juvenile pyromaniac onto the headmaster's wife. By the time they come to live in this house, if they ever do, the Days will have settled down to work for someone else."

"No, they won't. Mrs. Whitestone will fix it. But will the headmaster be allowed to live in this house?"

"After forty years at the school, they ought to donate it to him on his retirement. I'll put it to the school governors."

"You and I aren't connected with the school. Why should we expect to live in this house?"

"We'll move in when your brother moves out. To keep it warm for the retiring headmaster. We've got to live somewhere until our house is ready."

"We could live at Brighton."

"No. I'm going to stay here and keep an eye on all the workmen. Why don't you sell the Brighton house?"

"Because we're going to use it when Leo and Joshua and the twins want to do some sea bathing."

"We're going to need servants. Why hand the Days over to the —"

"We're fully staffed."

"We are?"

"Yes. We've got Mrs. Swayne as cook and Mrs. Lingford to do the housework."

"Does Mrs. Swayne know she's going to cook for us?"

"Not yet. Now will you go away?"

"Yes. But first I want to ask you something."

"What about?"

"About what the headmaster was saying at dinner the other night — which, in effect, was that all the Downing money had come from the town, and it was time the Downings gave some of it back. I want to try to do some of the things that were suggested. But it'll take a lot of money, and as you're marrying me, you ought to have a say in how I spend it. Will you mind seeing it rolling away?"

"You won't give away the house?"

"No."

"Or the farm?"

"No."

"Then that's all right. Good night."

"What's the hurry? We're alone; we're in love."

"You've got to be up early tomorrow."

"What for?"

"You've got to see that Maurice and Freddie check out of the hotel. Then you can ring me, and Julian and I can relax."

"Can I have a nice hot drink before I go home?"

"I suppose so. I'll make it."

"Stay where you are. It would take twenty minutes. I'll give up the hot drink and take the twenty minutes just as we are. Now close your eyes and start counting."

The draw for the Christmas hamper took place the following week. After making her usual annual inquiries, Geraldine had discovered that the oldest inhabitant was a retired grocer with the somewhat unusual name of Mr. Featherweight, who had retired from business thirty years ago. Now ninety-eight, he was frail of body but still clear in mind. His wheelchair was brought into his small parlour, and his grandchildren, ranging in age from twenty to forty, stood round it. On a table in a corner stood the large, overflowing Christmas hamper, decorated with holly. A few spectators crowded in to watch the proceedings.

Geraldine, holding a small canvas bag, addressed the host.

"Mr. Featherweight, we all think it's extremely kind of you to let us come here today. The money collected this year, as you may have seen from the local newspaper, has exceeded all previous years' collections."

There was a brief spatter of applause. When it had died down, Geraldine continued.

"In this bag —"

She paused once more; Henry and Natalie had arrived, and the spectators made a narrow gangway for them.

"In this bag are the numbers given to all the people who subscribed to the fund. In the book which my sister is holding are the names of the subscribers and the number that each one was given. I am going to ask you, Mr. Featherweight, to draw a number out of the bag and hold it up so that everybody here can see it."

This request was relayed to the old man by several of his grandchildren. Geraldine approached and held out the bag. Mr. Featherweight put in a hand and, after considerable fumbling, withdrew it and held up a number.

"Eighteen. Number eighteen has won," announced Geraldine. "Now we shall look in the book and see who the lucky winner is. Clarice, will you find number eighteen?"

Clarice opened the book, ran her finger down a page and then spoke.

"Number eighteen: Miss Geraldine Downing."

A murmur — disappointment or congratulation — ran round the room. Geraldine clasped her hands and spoke joyfully.

"Oh, what a splendid surprise! Lucky, lucky me! Thank you, Mr. Featherweight. And thank you all for coming here to watch the draw. I'd also like to thank all the people who contributed so generously to the fund. Now we mustn't tire Mr. Featherweight. I suggest we all say good-bye and thank him again for his kindness. May I ask him to accept part of my lucky draw?"

She walked to the hamper, picked out a very small can of peas and presented them to the old man. Applause greeted this generous gesture, and the visitors made their way into the narrow passage and so to the street. Geraldine turned to Henry.

"Henry, we have a taxi waiting outside — could I ask you to carry out the hamper? I'm so glad that you and Natalie were able to come and see the draw. I wish you could have won the prize." She was at the door. "Come along, Clarice."

But Clarice still had the book open and was looking at the numbers and muttering under her breath. She looked up with a frown.

"I don't understand, Geraldine. Look, there's —"

"That's all right, Clarice dear. Say good-bye to Mr. Featherweight."

Reluctantly Clarice made her farewell and followed her sister down the narrow little passage. Natalie was behind her; Henry, with the hamper, brought up the rear.

Outside the house Clarice spoke in a tone of resentment.

"There's a mistake," she said. "You got it last year."

"Yes, dear. Now let's go home."

"But number eighteen —"

"You're keeping the taxi waiting, Clarice."

"But it wasn't your turn. It was my turn."

"Don't *harp*, Clarice dear. Thank you for putting in the hamper, Henry. Good-bye. Good-bye, Natalie. I hope we shall see you both at our next concert. Come, Clarice."

Clarice, muttering, got into the taxi. Her sister followed her; the taxi drove away. Henry and Natalie walked slowly to Henry's car, in which they had left the twins.

"Pretty little ceremony," Henry observed.

Natalie was at the car door, staring absently at the twins.

"Did Geraldine win the hamper last year?" she asked.

259

"Yes. Wasn't she lucky to win it again?"

"Very lucky. Who won it the year before that?"

"Let me see . . . I think . . . yes, it was Clarice."

"And the year before that?"

"I think . . . yes, Geraldine."

"Hasn't anyone ever remarked on their extraordinary run of luck?"

"Not out loud." Ignoring the bystanders, he took her into his arms and kissed her lingeringly. "When I become the oldest inhabitant," he promised, "the winning number I draw out will be yours."

We hope you have enjoyed this Large Print book. Other G.K. Hall & Co. or Chivers Press Large Print books are available at your library or directly from the publishers.

For more information about current and up-coming titles, please call or write, without obligation, to:

G.K. Hall & Co.
P.O. Box 159
Thorndike, Maine 04986 USA
Tel. (800) 257-5157

OR

Chivers Press Limited
Windsor Bridge Road
Bath BA2 3AX
England
Tel. (0225) 335336

All our Large Print titles are designed for easy reading, and all our books are made to last.